The Death of H. L. Hix

The Death of H. L. Hix

H. L. Hix

Translated by H. L. Hix

Edited, and with an Introduction by H. L. Hix

About the Author

He *knows* it is an exaggeration, but still H. L. Hix finds the report of his death plausible.

About the Editor

All the king's horses and all the king's men couldn't put H. L. Hix together again.

About the Translator

Ev'n from the tomb the voice of H. L. Hix cries.

Contents

Introduction

Because he was of an age to have been educated in an ineptly-gendered literary canon, H. L. Hix would have had in his head for his whole adult life the lines that open and close T. S. Eliot's "East Coker": "In my beginning is my end" and "In my end is my beginning."[1] He must have loved the irony (could he even have *planned* it?) that the books that open and close his own oeuvre corroborate Eliot's lines. If H. L. Hix's first book, about "the death of the author,"[2] anticipated this his last book, about the death of *an* author, himself, then in H. L. Hix's beginning was his end, and in his end was his beginning.

Writing about that first book (in an essay so witty it kills me to read it), David Foster Wallace observes that "Hix de-

---

1   In *The Complete Poems and Plays, 1909-1950* (Harcourt, Brace and World, 1971), pp. 123, 129. Since his canon-cocksure professors had packed the old boys into H. L. Hix's head tightly as shot in a shell, surely he would have made the further association of Eliotic echolocation of end in beginning and beginning in end with Nietzschean eternal recurrence and *amor fati*, giving any report of his death as a way to reiterate Zarathustra's rhetorical question "Was *that* life?" and thus to imply Zarathustra's exclamations "Well then! Once more!"

2   *Morte d'Author: An Autopsy* (Temple Univ. Press, 1990). That book's beginning was its end, too. Hix held degrees in philosophy: if not in the seminar room then at least in the halls he would have overheard enough to relish the irony that his treatise on the author's nature (the conclusion of which discusses Hume) fell, like Hume's *Treatise of Human Nature*, "dead-born from the press," establishing the precedent each later H. L. Hix book would follow, of exciting not a murmur.

stroys the author in order to save him."[3] This, too, offered a delicious irony, in that Hix, who in one way (though in *only* one way) outlived Wallace, ultimately verified the truth that needs no verification, namely that we all of us, authors or not, sooner or later are destroyed, and no one of us is saved by that destruction. No preemption is possible; no kind or quantity of preliminary destruction precludes or averts ultimate destruction. Like every other human, H. L. Hix proved in the end less destroyer than destroyed.

The mere fact of his having been brought up on syllabi skewed toward the Anglocentric and selected from long centuries of the androcentric would give grounds enough for guessing that H. L. Hix had in his head not only those two if-you-say-sos from a certain Thomas Stearns but also this way-with-words from one especially well-known William:

> I am myself indifferent honest; but yet I could accuse me of such things that it were better my mother had not borne me: I am very proud, revengeful, ambitious, with more offences at my beck than I have thoughts to put them in, imagination to give them shape, or time to act them in. What should such fellows as I do crawling between earth and heaven? We are arrant knaves, all; believe none of us.[4]

3   "Greatly Exaggerated," in *A Supposedly Fun Thing I'll Never Do Again* (Little, Brown and Co., 1997), p. 144. This essay, too, established a precedent. H. L. Hix briefly believed that being reviewed by David Foster Wallace would boost his book, but sales figures soon burst his bubble. To describe Hix's response to the repeatedly splashless reception of his books, those close to him, saying it was similar for each title, use such terms as "maudlin" and "self-pitying."

4   *Hamlet*, III, i. H. L. Hix took seriously enough the charge Hamlet issues here, to "believe none of us," to have sketched out a bullet-point plan for a book he never wrote, on the unreliable narra-

H. L. Hix would have had by heart that Shakespeare,[5] and (with the Athenocentrism instilled in him as sturdy stylobate to secure that intricate Anglocentric entablature) would have taken to heart this more often merely taken-for-granted Aristotle: "The difference between historian and poet is not that the one writes in prose and the other in verse, but that the one details what has happened and the other what may happen."[6]

---

tor in philosophical works, asking what follows if philosophy stands (or if one stands philosophy) not on the shoulders of Socrates, for whom wisdom can be flushed from ignorance as easily as pheasant from stubble, but on the shoulders of the Cretan Liar, for whom truth and untruth don't pull apart. How (he asks in that outline) does one's reading of that series of footnotes to Plato change, if the Er-text is not an ur-text and Plato's only a footnote to Zeno? What if philosophy consists not in waving aside the flimsy scrim of the physical to bathe in the bright metaphysical light that anyway shines through it, but in bumping repeatedly against an unyielding wall of paradox?

5   To Hamlet's worry that it would have been objectively better had his mother never borne him, he would have added Yeats's worry that any youthful mother, could she see her son with "sixty or more winters on his head," would find it subjectively better, too, not to have so shrilly shrieked for something that would so surely shrivel. H. L. Hix's sixty winters did more to second Plato's spume-upon-a-ghostly-paradigm-of-things supposition than to compensate his mother for the pang of his birth.

6   *Poetics*, 1451b. If Aristotle were writing today, he might contrast different genres. The celebrity kiss-and-tell spills what's none of your business, the memoir spells out what would be better left unsaid. For its part, H. L. Hix's own poetics, as is demonstrated in his late work *Demonstrategy* (Etruscan Press, 2019), assigned a more inclusive list of modalities to poetry, which on his view is able to detail not only what *may* happen but also, for instance, what *must* happen, what *might have* happened, what *would* happen, and so on. That is to say, poetry, on H. L. Hix's view, is sufficiently protean to become hypothesis, prophecy, lamentation, prayer, and on and on.

What anyone would have grounds to suspect, scholars give evidence to support, because in H. L. Hix's papers has been found a page of notes, handwritten in turquoise ink on the verso of a photocopied sheet on which those two passages, the Shakespeare and the Aristotle, appear in typescript on the recto. One plausible hypothesis, suggested in part by those passages' placement on the page, holds that Hix intended to post them as epigraphs to the present volume.[7] The extant manuscript, in the condition in which it was left in H. L. Hix's papers, does not present the paired passages as epigraphs; consequently, I have not done so in this edition. No epigraphs there, none here. So convinced am I, though, that it was Hix's intention to give those passages as glosses for this book, that I invite the reader to receive them as such, positioning them mentally where they do not stand textually.[8]

This edition, ably translated from the original by H. L. Hix himself, contains all the extant chapters. Hix did not date

---

7 Scholarly consensus offers the epigraph theory as *one* plausible hypothesis, but I myself find it *the most* plausible hypothesis of any so far proposed. The turquoise-tinted notes (in water-based ink that bleeds through the flimsy copier paper on which the passages are printed) consist of ideas toward the present volume: ways in which H. L. Hix suffered, nightmares H. L. Hix endured, stories Gary Simm told, and so on. Without making too much of it, I do point out here that "maudlin" and "self-pitying," applied by others to describe H. L Hix's response to the reception of his books, applies equally well to his notes for the present work. It would be only fitting if he *did* intend to post on this work's lintel a lament from that most histrionic hero, Hamlet.

8 If I were H. L. Hix, I'd add, from the Y-chromosome-crammed chrestomathy so early and indelibly imprinted on his memory, a third epigraph, this kernel of Keats: "I have been half in love with easeful Death." Even a fourth, a whiff of Whitman: "I will show that nothing can happen more beautiful than death." But that's just me.

drafts, so, where more than one draft of a chapter exists, I have included here only the longest.[9] The sole exception to this principle is the chapter describing in detail the shed. I chose the version included here over a significantly longer version, because that version's additional length took the form of an extensive (possibly even *exhaustive*) inventory of items stored in the shed. Surely I am, of all readers of H. L. Hix's work, the most inclined to indulge his various writerly excesses, but even I found that particular list a step or two past superfluous.[10]

---

9   Employing this principle constitutes a guess that the sole surviving manuscript was an early draft. We know that in H. L. Hix's prose writing (though *only* in his prose; his poetry is a different story), earlier drafts are primarily additive, later drafts primarily subtractive. An editor who believed this work was well along in the process of composition and revision, then, would be obliged to choose the *shorter* versions. Ironically, the editorial approach I have taken presents a long version but (by its premise that these must be early drafts) implies that the version presented would be better if it were shorter.

10   Prominent among H. L. Hix's writerly excesses, I recognize, is his love of lists, so he might well have intended to keep the longer version. Nevertheless, I have kept the shorter, on the grounds that no rational adult could possibly find, in *reading* a list of household items and gardening utensils stored in a shed, the same self-indulgent pleasure that H. L. Hix took in *writing* that list. (A shed is a shed! You put stuff there instead of in the house because it is *not* important stuff. Making a list of unimportant stuff might be fun, at least in the qualified way piecing together a jigsaw puzzle is fun, but reading such a list is no more fun than watching someone else put a puzzle together.) Former students recount an incident from a class H. L. Hix and the artist Adriane Herman team-taught early in their careers. During one critique session, when Hix described the work under discussion as "self-indulgent," Herman is said to have challenged him: "What's wrong with self-indulgence?" H. L. Hix wrestled with that question the rest of his working life, but his reluctantly-acquired openness to self-indulgence does not oblige his editors.

That decision is, I believe, the only lapse in my otherwise unwavering commitment to editorial minimalism. Hewing to my intention to keep my judgments of taste to myself, I have worked hard to avoid being interventionist in my capacity as editor.[11]

The order of the chapters here is unique to this edition. It seems clear that the single surviving manuscript is incomplete, as how could it not be: it was found in two manila folders, labeled simply "1" and "4,"[12] but no "2" or "3" has turned

---

11   I have avoided being interventionist, but I have chipped away at a few others of H. L. Hix's writerly excesses, in addition to the love of lists. For instance, his (self-indulgent) oneirophilia. A great many of the loose sheets in folders 1 and 4 contained accounts of dreams. I have included here only a handful of those accounts, by no means all of them, on the grounds that the reader quickly gets the idea that H. L. Hix's dreams got crazier and more frequent as his health deteriorated; no need to belabor the point. Including all the dream accounts would distract from other, more definitive aspects of H. L. Hix's decline and fall.

One other writerly leak over which I have placed an editorial patch is patronymics. I can't stop H. L. Hix from stealing Tolstoy's story, but H. L. Hix gives it as a lament that he has to die *and* that he doesn't get a death of his own: I get it. I'm as upset as he is. I don't need Russian names to remind me that the life I'm living and the death I'm dying are someone else's, not my own. To spare the reader H. L. Hix's heavy-handedness, I have Anglicized the names that in the manuscript are Russian: for the manuscript's Gerasim I have substituted Gary Simm; Praskovya Fyodorovna in the manuscript becomes Priscilla Frederickson in this edition; and so on.

12   The numbers are written larger than H. L. Hix's usual handwriting, in sharpie rather than pen or pencil, so they are plainly visible, but because they are inscribed on the front of each folder, not on its tab, they would have been useful only in identifying folders stacked, not folders filed. And in fact these two folders were found, at H. L. Hix's death, laid flat atop a messy pile (not stood upright as part of a tidy row), among the misery of manila folders and mucilage that dolored his desk.

up. Of course it is possible that the numbers have nothing to do with this manuscript,[13] but so numerous and so large were the gaps in the narrative that no scholar has seriously challenged the obvious assumption that there were two more folders, possibly with more material than the surviving folders held.[14] We have firm grounds, then, to regard the manuscript as incomplete, but we have no good reason to assume of the surviving pages that they were preserved in an order intended for publication. Indeed, so abrupt are the breaks between some of the sections, so difficult is it to discern in the sheets as they followed one another in the folders any continuity or narrative arc, that one must assume so unsatisfying a sequence *could not* have been final.

The sheets in folders 1 and 4 confirm what we know from other manuscripts, namely that H. L. Hix worked by scribbling in ink on printed pages, keying in the handwritten revisions, printing the updated version, and so on, over and over. The earlier pages in folder 1 are much more heavily marked than later pages, so the likelihood is that the manuscript pages of this text were arranged in the folders according to how intensively they had been worked, rather than according to the sequence in which they were intended ultimately to appear. I have taken this uncertainty about the basis for the order of the sheets in each sheaf as permission to make a small number of

---

13   We know that H. L. Hix re-used folders over and over, occasionally revising the labeling to indicate the current contents, but more often not.

14   Remarkably, no scholar to date has proposed the obvious possibility that there were even *more* folders. (Why assume that folder 4 is final? Why could there not be a 5, even a 6? It would be just the sort of poetic justice H. L. Hix loved, if parts of the story of the life he was losing were lost.)

mostly minor adjustments.[15]

15 For example, the section I have placed first was buried in
the middle of folder 1, and the section I have placed last was not
even *in* folder 4. Without compromising my global principle of
editorial non-intervention, I have taken authorial inconsistencies as
warrant for other minor, local editorial liberties. For instance, the
sections are less clearly divided in manuscript than in this final published text. As editors have regularized Dickinson's dashes, so I have
normalized into bullets H. L. Hix's erratic ways of marking breaks.
That is to say, the division into sections and the sequencing of those
sections both are more mine than his.

The chapter titles and the text on the title pages of the chapters
has no basis in the manuscript, per se. If my limiting the length of the
what's-in-the-shed list inhibits one of H. L Hix's writerly excesses,
my imposition of chapter divisions and chapter heads fulfills another
of his excesses. He was forever structuring whole sequences of poems, whole books even, by analogy with ways of structuring individual
poems. It hardly matters that I myself am skeptical of the principle
behind this practice, namely that if structure participates in meaning
at the level of a poem (as, say, octave/turn/sestet does in a sonnet) and
in other art forms (as composition does in a David painting or as ex-
position/development/recapitulation in a Bach fugue), then it does so,
too, at larger literary scales than individual poems. I say don't lay out
a prelude and fugue for every key, just give me a melody I can whistle.
What concern have I for complexity? I have trouble enough trying to
manage the simple. But that wasn't H. L. Hix's way.

Knowing that, had he lived, he would have imposed some stul-
tifying, artificial structure on the material, I have imposed on it the
twelve-chapter arrangement. It is not anything he actually did, but it
is just the sort of thing he would have done. For warrant, I appeal to
the Aristotle cited above: I'm here mostly as historian, but in making
the chapters I play poet. On this principle, the chapter heads need
not be anything H. L. Hix *did write*, to be the sort of thing he *might
have written*. If he were alive to see it, surely he would affirm, for
instance, letting the Devils of Hell answer the Sphinx. He wouldn't
merely approve: he would wish he'd thought of it himself.

I confess I was proud of myself over the chapter titles. If I were
one to boast, I'd claim to have made up a whole new form I'd name
a derian: an abridged abecederian, one without the abc.

Some scholars have expressed surprise that the manuscript exists only in hard copy. Wouldn't the material from folders 2 and 3 be on a hard drive? Couldn't it be recovered? The fact, though, however unfortunate for literary posterity, is easy to explain. Many quirks marked H. L. Hix's peculiar and ambivalent relationship to digital technology (he wrote programs early, in FORTRAN on stacks of punch cards, but he never later took a shine to Photoshop; he was among the first consumers on the planet to purchase a Macintosh,[16] among the last to own an iPhone, first to email, last to text, early to blog, late to tweet). Refusal to back up his hard drive was just one among those many quirks.[17] The laptop on which Hix composed these pages was the property of his employer, so when (despite its age[18]) the university reclaimed it, all of H. L. Hix's digital files were lost. We have this manuscript because he had printed a hard copy; there may have been other texts on which H. L. Hix was working before illness and death

---

16   As surely as it would date him to discover he had ventured west in a Conestoga on the Oregon Trail, it dates him to disclose that he bought his first computer in the days of floppy discs and black-and-white monitors and dot matrix and 128K RAM, when the alternative was an Atari word processor. This wasn't merely before thumbs-up emojis and internet rabbit holes; this was even before Crystal Quest or Tetris.

17   I use the word "refusal" advisedly: there is reason to think that not making back-ups was a conscious *decision*, not just laziness, though *why* Hix made that decision remains a mystery. Rumors that his drop of philosophy is condensed in the cloud circulate as loosely as sightings of ivory-billed woodpeckers and Bigfoot, and are no more plausible.

18   At the time of Hix's death, his computer was eight years old, a veritable antique, older in computer years than he himself was in human years.

overtook him,[19] but we have no way to know.

So much for the manuscript history of *The Death of H. L. Hix*.[20] Its genre, themes, and meaning, its place in H. L. Hix's extensive oeuvre, all are less clear. Selling it as fiction would depend on a fib: there *are* resemblances to persons living and dead, deny it though the publishers' lawyers insist.[21] But no more is it memoir: precious little of the factual appears in this account. *This* picture doesn't reach right out to any reality: H. L. Hix is an unreliable narrator, as he was an unreliable person, an unreliable existent. He knew not to trust himself; the reader is here warned not to trust him. Nowhere in the sheaf of notes does Hix himself identify this work with an existing genre. I propose that it invents a new genre, the wicked twin that until now autobiography didn't know it had, automortography.

By addressing death, this work is drawn into certain inevitable thematic concerns. The H. L. Hix portrayed here keeps

---

19 Anecdotal evidence suggests that Hix flitted inconsistenly from project to project, a pattern his papers confirm. He left behind numerous unpublished manuscripts. To let a single example stand for the rest, one folder from one unsteady stack of folders left in H. L. Hix's cluttered study contains the only verse translation into English of all the poems of Fray Luis de León. It's not the *completed* projects that concern us here, though: he left *un*completed a great many more projects than he completed. Before falling ill, he had been letting on to friends that he was well along in a large-scale, thousand-page poetry project called *Glasswing*, but no hard copy has been found. Because this sounds to me so much like self-mythologizing, I advise the reader to believe it when you see it.

20 The title, too, by the way, is my addition; no title appears on the manuscript itself.

21 Absent such resemblances, the point of stories would be what? Though in this case the most notable resemblance is less to persons themselves (H. L. Hix could be anybody, was nobody) than to the inevitability with which persons living become persons dead.

trying desperately to prove himself exceptional: keeps trying
to live with integrity according to his highest moral principles;
to live an examined life washed clean of self-deception; to re-
ject injustice and contest institutional forms of structural vio-
lence; and so on. His death, though, both the manner of his
dying and the brute fact that he died, reveals those attempts
as futile: it proves H. L. Hix in every way *un*exceptional. As
for meaning, I must remain mum: I can hardly claim to have
extracted meaning from a text that so elaborately narrates the
draining-away of meaning and so emphatically depicts mean-
inglessness as ultimate.

How those perplexities of genre, theme, and meaning fold
into their sister perplexities in others of H. L. Hix's works
is difficult to ascertain. It is *not* difficult, though, to discern,
throughout H. L. Hix's works, premonitions of his death. *This*
work is anticipated in all of H. L. Hix's prior works. (In his
end is his beginning, in his beginning his end.) I began this
introduction by referring to his blatantly premonitory first
book, taking the death of the author as its explicit subject matter. But his death, far from being confined to that one book, is
everywhere in his work: it's a veritable obsession. Here I note
only a few examples:[22]

> • The preoccupation pervades his later prose. After
> *Morte d'Author*, his next book presents his death with
> more subtlety, but just as surely. These four declara-
> tions, for instance, appear far apart in the book, but
> how else read them, when they are set side by side,
> than as self-referential presentiments? "Thought is a
> form of grief"; "A lament is always the mask of a dif-

---

22   You won't catch *me* indulging in H. L. Hix's excessive list-
love!

ferent lament hidden behind it"; "Only as the story of a death can the story of a life interest us"; "Philosophy is always autobiography, but never the autobiography it looks like."[23]

Or, again, in his first collection of essays on poetry, he vows that, in defiance of his inevitable failure to live up to his own ideals, "I will, as they say in what passes for poetry where I come from, die trying."[24] Which is just what, apparently, he understands himself to be doing when, near the end of a later essay collection, he describes himself, in the third person, as having "left even himself" and as "scatter[ing] small formalities like birdseed, / hoping only briefly to see, / to tempt a few timid hungry fragments of his / fugitive brightly-colored life."[25]

• Even in H. L. Hix's translations of the work of others, he proved unwilling — or unable — to stop himself from insinuating his own death. Why else make half of his last poetry collection translations, and

---

23 *Spirits Hovering Over the Ashes: Legacies of Postmodern Theory* (SUNY Press, 1995). The passages quoted here are drawn from pp. 9, 164, 165, and 191, respectively. One need not imagine that H. L. Hix *wrote* them with the present work in mind, to *read* them as applying to the present work, disturbing it and disturbed by it in turn. If this lament masks another lament, doesn't *that* lament mask yet another? How many layers of lament lurk behind this one? Is no lament ultimate? At what point should one let layered laments lie?

24 *As Easy As Lying: Essays on Poetry* (Etruscan Press, 2002), p. 6. I did briefly entertain the idea of taking *Die Trying* for the title of the present work, so that the title would at least be H. L. Hix's *words*, even if not his *choice*, but settled on the present title as (though not nearly so catchy) the more direct and plainspoken alternative.

25 *Lines of Inquiry* (Etruscan Press, 2011), p. 122.

translations taken from especially oracular ancients? Those oracle-workers, after all, were inclined to such assertions as these: "Awake, we see only death; asleep, only sleep"; "Living dead waking sleeping young old, same thing"; "What awaits humans at death defies what they expect or imagine"; "What will disappear, must. Already has. / The dead do not live, nor do the living die"; "No hiding, no hidden, no place to hide"; "You are worrying about the wrong death"; "What you expect has happened already."[26]

Similarly, in his penultimate poetry collection, Hix's selections from Greek tragedies, translated in the "Erinyeneutics" section of that book, purport to have been chosen for their depicting anger, but a disproportionate number also remark how darkly the shadow of his own death looms already over H. L. Hix. Why choose, for example, from the whole of Euripides' *Phoenician Women*, the four lines in which Polyneices asks his mother and sister to bury him in his homeland, to "assert my claim to just so much earth / from my birthplace, though I have lost my home."[27]

• The pattern is most pronounced in H. L. Hix's

---

26   Each quoted passage comes from *Rain Inscription* (Etruscan Press, 2017), some translating words anciently attributed to Herakleitos, others words attributed to Jesus. The passages appear on pp. 37, 39, 42, 46, 50, 53, and 76, respectively.

27   *American Anger: An Evidentiary* (Etruscan Press, 2016), p. 145. And this is not to mention H. L. Hix's edition and translation of the gospel, which assembled sources that so strongly emphasized Jesus' premonitions of (as the pronoun appears there) *xer* death.

poetry.[28] It doesn't take much effort to identify the murder victim in the long narrative poem that opens H. L. Hix's selected poems with H. L. Hix himself, and after making that identification, it's no stretch to connect H. L. Hix also with whoever dies in the other "anchor" poem.[29] Never mind that he closes that same volume of selected poems with a valediction, itself ending with the question "What truth waves us goodbye at this window?" Nowhere, though, is the presentiment clearer than in the narrative sequence called "The Well-Tempered Clavier," one premise of which is that the protagonist (so much like H. L. Hix himself that any reader would identify the two) has a premonition of his imminent death in a car wreck.[30]

Obsession with his own death does not entail that H. L. Hix was undeceived about his own mortality, but the obses-

---

28   If I were less concerned to maintain editorial neutrality, I would say the pattern is most *egregious* in his poetry.

29   Indeed, the connection is especially apt. One can say of either case, that poem or the death of H. L. Hix, that we know *someone* dies, but we don't know *who*.

30   The two anchor poems mentioned here display another of H. L. Hix's writerly excesses, a propensity to allow himself liberties with titles, in this case the liberty of inordinate length: they are entitled, respectively, "Even Be It Built of Boards Planed by Hand and Joined Without Nails, Yet May a Barn Burn" and "Though What Falls Fall Hard to Hard Ground, Yet May Birds Nest Among Flowers, Flowers Grow in the Sky." The whole of "The Well-Tempered Clavier," not only its title, illustrates one of the excesses criticized above, namely his *un*tempered trust in the capacity of structure to deliver meaning, and his consequent tendency to over-architecture all his poetry. The selected from which I cite the poems mentioned here is *First Fire, Then Birds: Obsessionals 1985-2010* (Etruscan Press, 2010).

sion does run through everything he wrote. The pieces might be scattered through his works, but the puzzle picture isn't hard to see.

Let me here put to rest one wholly unfounded rumor. A myth has grown up around this book: that it was only *after* H. L. Hix had started writing it that the symptoms it chronicles began, as if the illness that killed him were a textual effect,[31] the failure of his kidney and heart akin to stigmata.[32] As if he first wrote the story of his death and only then (*because* he had written the story) experienced it. This view is a form of magical thinking, and I advise the reader against succumbing to it.[33]

This is the point at which I am supposed to write that space limitations preclude my outlining the full extent of H. L. Hix's rich and complex legacy, a labor I leave to later scholars. Excusing myself in that way, though, would presume too much,[34] so, instead, I leave to later scholars the liberty to assign themselves their own labors, as I leave to readers the autonomy to make of the following pages what they will. Establishing the text was my job; interpreting it, I leave to you. In H. L. Hix's end, reader, is your beginning.

H. L. Hix

------

31   Here the reader is reminded that "there is nothing outside of death" is actually a clumsy mistranslation of "il n'y a pas de hors-mort," which is more aptly rendered "there is no outside-death."

32   Or a solipsistic variant of the hyperempathy Octavia Butler imagines in her fiction.

33   Though I tender this advice without denying the broader metaphysical premise behind the advised-against, that in the beginning was the Word, and the Word was with Death, and the Word was Death.

34   It would presume, for instance, that H. L. Hix's legacy *is* rich and complex, indeed that H. L. Hix leaves any legacy at all.

death [From the Old Norse *deyja*, to die.] The event of dying, or the condition of being dead. Event, as when Milton's Eve declares of her Adam, "So dear I love him, that with him all deaths / I could endure, without him live no life"; condition, as when, in *Wives and Daughters*, Gaskell's Squire stands "in dumb dismay, touched in spite of himself by the death-in-life of one so young."

A mathematician might add, to the many already offered, yet another proof of the Pythagorean Theorem; an argument doesn't have to show us something *new*, to show us something *anew*. Here H. L. Hix adds, to the countless many already given by others, yet one more demonstration that to narrate an event of death is to lament the condition.

•

What goes on four legs in the morning and two at noon, but by early evening lies bedridden?

•

All animals are dying, but some are more dying than others.

$$\bullet\ \bullet\ \bullet$$

In the first-floor coffee room of Hoyt Hall, on the campus of the University of Wyoming, a few senior literature faculty were chatting. The English Department was about to meet in the conference room just down the hall, and these colleagues had convened here a little before the hour, to pass together that temporal epitome of academia: a stretch of boredom anticipating the onset of drudgery. Better to wait here among equals than in the meeting room itself, where assistant professors and composition faculty and even lecturers would be already gathering.

The professorial palaver turned to consequences for the department of the latest university hiring freeze and strategic planning initiative. Current cutbacks and five-year plans seemed always to be paired, bookends placed at the limits of administrative competence, to prop it up. Melanie Tolliver (known to the wider scholarly world for her monographs on William McGonagall, but in the building nicknamed "Pistons" because her stride on short but sturdy legs was such that when she stomped from her office to scold the Chair, as so often she did, everyone in Hoyt could hear) insisted that if she could just insinuate herself onto the college-wide committee, she could push through into the new strategic plan a Ph.D. program for the department. Her voice rose and she grew increasingly animated as she approached her conclusion: "With our strength in eighteenth century," she boasted, eyes raised to heaven like an ecstatic saint, "we'd make waves in the MLA." Altogether ignoring Tolliver's declaration, Kirk

Stiles (who prided himself on being praised every semester in student evals for his practice of pausing to weep when reading passages from *Pride and Prejudice* aloud to the susceptibles in his sophomore survey) was about to say what he always said, regardless of the subject being discussed, namely that the department had been without a Miltonist for *years*.

Suddenly, though, he stopped scrolling on the screen he held. "Colleagues," he intoned, "H. L. Hix is dead."

"Really?" Melanie Tolliver, returning from her reverie, fairly shrieked. She even paused in her pacing back and forth across the small room.

"Here, see for yourself," Stiles said, not to Tolliver but to Dash Westover, who hadn't entered the conversation yet because he'd been staring, vexed, into his Princeton mug, trying to decide whether this coffee was *so* badly pot-scalded that he should go to the trouble of brewing a new pot, in violation of his principle that keeping coffee fresh is the secretary's job. As if it weren't bad enough that he had to suffer coffee bought in bulk and brewed in a drip machine with a basket filter, so inferior to the foil-packaged whole-bean small-batch premium varietal coffee he fresh-ground and french-pressed for himself at home. If he didn't live at altitude, he'd do his own roasting, only Kona beans except for an occasional batch of Blue Mountain to keep his palate refined and alert. Nor was scorched coffee the only indignity he suffered in this uncivilized outpost: he still held a grudge against the previous Chair, for buying Dell desktops all around with department funds but then refusing him reimbursement for a broad-nibbed Pelikan M1000 that would serve his research agenda, and outlast all those microprocessing planned obscolences.

Stiles made a quick thumb-and-finger swipe to magnify one passage from the obituaries page of the *Laramie Boomerang*, and held out the tablet. Westover skimmed the notice on the screen, quickly enough to catch only these portions:

H. L. Hix, 59, of Laramie, died Sunday, February… , at his home, after a prolonged illness. He was born November… , in Stillwater, Oklahoma…

He is survived by…

A memorial service celebrating his life will be held at his home at 5 p.m. on Friday, February…

In lieu of flowers, the family requests that memorial contributions be made to…

The photo accompanying the text was ancient, a head shot taken at the time of H. L. Hix's hire, showing him with long-fallen-out-of-fashion glasses and an even-then-years-out-of-style haircut. Anything more recent would have depicted thicker glasses (trifocals now, no longer bi-), and thinner hair (faded farther, from salt-and-pepper to simply salt). Since the day of that photo, H. L. Hix had not worn the diagonally-striped two-tone tie whose deep-dimpled half windsor was visible in the portrait, but it still adorned his closet at the time of his death. Only the fact of cremation complemented by a memorial service, rather than an open-casket funeral with interment to follow, spared Priscilla Frederickson the decision whether to have that very tie buried tight around the neck of H. L. Hix's corpse.

•

H. L. Hix had been a member of the English Department once upon a time, and those assembled, fixtures in Hoyt Hall for decades now, had known him well. He'd been sick, though, since the summer, so none of them had seen him for some time, and anyway he'd been reassigned several years ago from English to Philosophy, so his office was across the way, in Ross. The buildings were adjacent, barely thirty steps from door to door across a narrow one-way service drive, but the move might as well have been to Tierra del Fuego or the Hebrides: it meant no more passing conversations standing at the mailboxes, waiting for the photocopier, or facing the wall at adjacent urinals.

Since no one in the room had interacted recently with H. L. Hix himself, the conversation concerned only his position, not his person. About the former, each discussant had a professorial opinion; about the latter, who could say.

"Will they replace him, you think?"

"No, of course not. This place? This travesty of the ideals of higher education is trying to erase the humanities altogether. They'll hold a little celebration in Old Main with confetti and punch and party horns, the administration will be so glad he's gone."

"*Would* be glad, if they could be brought to notice."

"It's not only Old Main. Even his department will be relieved. It's all analytic, and he taught continental. H. L. Hix was an inconvenience, the umbrella you tote around all day even though it's not going to rain. His absence spares their majors a few frivolities, distractions from serious study of serious philosophy. I heard he'd gone completely around the bend: before he took sick, he'd taken to teaching Sara Ahmed and Sayak Valencia and Octavia Butler and Wendy Brown. Imagine. That's what happens when you lose your grip on the great books."

Melanie Tolliver blurted out, "That's what happens when the great books lose their grip on you!" The others ignored her.

"It's good he's gone, like finally getting rid of a lingering infection."

"I heard he'd hung an evil-eye amulet over his office door, and turned vegan. It's a wonder he hadn't started wearing tie-dyed T-shirts and hemp-rope sandals. He always was a little out of step."

"The Dean will be happy to have that salary line back. Pay a per-course pittance or two, and pocket the rest."

"Too bad he bailed on English, though. We could have made a strong case for keeping the line and advertising for a Miltonist."

•

Conversation about H. L. Hix's death did not extend beyond its minor implications for the university and thus indirectly for their own positions. Each party to the conversation, though, experienced the usual relief that accompanies learning of another's death: thank god *he* died, not me. No one breached decorum by saying it aloud, but to each person present, the meaning of H. L. Hix's death was: I am still alive.

The Dean will skim his salary, but I am still alive. The Dean did not know H. L. Hix's name until one or another associate dean informed her that his line had opened up, but I am still alive. He never fit in on this campus, anyway, and I am still alive. Why they hired him in the first place I'll never know: he wasn't Phi Beta Kappa and he didn't have Ivy League credentials. But I am still alive. You couldn't call it scholarship, that fluff he wrote that never shows up in citations and wasn't published by respectable scholarly presses and that even the university's own library doesn't collect, and I am still alive. In a year, no one will remember he was ever here, and in two years not a single student walking the campus will have so much as heard his name, but I am still alive. Maybe someone will name a hundred-dollar scholarship or a departmental essay prize after him, but I wouldn't bet the farm on it, and I am still alive. Former students might express their sorrow with a few brief Facebook posts stippled with thumbs-down and sad-mouth emojis, but I am still alive. Many more people will swipe his obituary across a smart-phone screen than will scan any three consecutive pages from any one of his books, but I am still alive. His shirts and shoes and his elbow-worn herringbone blazer will show up at the thrift store, and the dog-eared trade paperbacks from his shelves will be lined spine-up on plywood folding tables at the library fundraiser, but I am still alive. If anyone asks why I wasn't at the memorial service, I'll say I had to be out of town. I am still alive. He's not in the ground yet and already they've emptied his office, but I am still alive. So much stuff he should have thrown away himself instead of leaving it for someone else to pitch: old desk copies and older files, old syllabi and older gradebooks, his cap and gown, comb-bound photocopied conference proceedings from the days before pdfs. But I am still alive. I bet someone kept his nice glass tea infuser, though. I could have used it, to replace the stained metal mesh strainer at my office; I am still alive.

If the Chair will stick to the agenda for a change, I can head out for a drink after this meeting. I am still alive.

•

Though he and his wife had shared a good laugh over the obituary's calling it "a memorial service celebrating his life," Kirk Stiles did attend, as propriety demanded. He drove to what had been H. L. Hix's home and parked at the curb, not far away. He'd made a point of first circling the block, to be sure he wasn't first to arrive.

As he walked from his car toward the house, Kirk shook his head over all the dubious decisions H. L. Hix had made. It was a mystery, he thought to himself, why anyone would choose to live in an old relic like this house, with all the maintenance problems from old pipes and wiring, and such small closets besides, here among shabby run-down rentals festering with undergraduates and in constant turnover, when there were subdivisions in town where the houses weren't so cramped and decrepit, and one's neighbors were other professors who could be counted on to stay the same from one semester to the next. Not far away, either. He himself could push the button on his garage door opener, get into his perfectly warm SUV, and drive to the lot in front of Hoyt in the time it would take H. L. Hix to scrape the thick crust of overnight ice from the windshield of his parked-on-the-street subcompact, or to risk the slick sidewalks and suffer the numbing gusts, going on foot.

H. L. Hix probably even shoveled his own sidewalks all winter, Stiles thought to himself, and then wondered who he'd hired to shovel them through his illness. "And what a noisy latch," he said to himself, though not out loud, as he shut the gate of the weather-wearied wooden fence to H. L. Hix's yard, its posts wobbly, its unpainted pickets all splitting or warping away from the rails.

Inside the house, Kirk Stiles felt himself at a loss for how he should properly act. As far as he knew, H. L. Hix hadn't been Christian or Jewish or Muslim, hadn't belonged to any religious community or practiced any faith. Should he cross himself? There wasn't an icon or altar to look at while doing so. This was a private home, not a church. Should he kneel? To *what?* He settled on leaning slightly forward and inclining his head a little, a demi-genuflection accompanied by an ambiguous gesture that took his hand past his heart. He felt others watching him from the corner of their eyes, but was sure that anyone would interpret this as decorous behavior, respectful but not eccentric. Those who thought he should cross himself would see him as having done so.

Even while he gestured, Stiles continued to scan the room. He hadn't been in H. L. Hix's home before, and was surprised at how little had been updated: it did have the nice high ceilings all these old hard-to-heat houses had, but the baseboards bore who knew how many layers of lead paint on them, when what they needed was just to be replaced; the hardwood floors were so scuffed and stained they must be as old as the house itself; the oriental rug was too rectangular for so square a room, and looked to be machine-made. He felt almost aghast: the rug was clearly synthetic, and probably spread directly over the floor itself, with no horse hair rug pad between. Lack of taste shows up in so many ways, Stiles thought to himself. The old cable connection (was there still such a *thing* as cable?) still stuck out from the wall: just the sort of thing that if this were his house he would have had someone in to take care of long ago.

Finally, he spotted, on a side table in one corner of the room, what must be the urn. He controlled his face, so as not to register his surprise at how *small* the urn was. A whole body, a whole life, and all that was left of H. L. Hix would fit into *that*. He imagined the clear plastic bag it enclosed, ashes the color and texture of so much bleached flour, secured by a gold-tone twisty-tie.

Kirk Stiles had just begun to worry how long the ceremony would drag on, since clearly, with so few chairs in the room, he would have to stand, when a woman's voice interrupted. "Thank you for coming." It was Priscilla Frederickson, the widow. He'd met her before, at department social functions, and always wondered what had first attracted her to H. L. Hix, and (the greater mystery) why she stayed with him. She had so much more personality than he'd had, so much more *presence.* Visible tattoos. Hair a different color every time he saw her. She went by "Prissy," and seemed to like sharing the name of an attitude. If the two of them were part of a pedimental sculpture from a Greek temple, Stiles thought to himself, she'd have been tall, stationed at the center, standing contrapposto with one arm raised, dressed in dramatic drapery, and H. L. Hix would have been cramped in an awkward crouch, cowering at one or the other corner. He'd known she had more charisma than H. L. Hix had, but still Stiles was more than a little taken aback by Priscilla Frederickson's clothing on this solemn occasion: skirt and blouse instead of a dress, the one charcoal rather than black, the other practically heather. He kept his composure, though, and performed what he knew decorum demanded of him in his role as one paying respects. He clasped her hands in his, and said, "I'm *so* sorry." Hearing his own words in so earnest a tone of sympathy, he was moved nearly to tears, and he thought that surely she was, too.

"Come with me," she said, directing him with a barely perceptible movement of her head, "there's something I have to ask you." He followed her into the next room. In this tiny, cramped house there wasn't a room far enough from the main living area to let them speak in true privacy, and this was the main bedroom, with guests' coats (the price of a house with no foyer and coat closet) not hung neatly but tossed in a heap on the bed. Stiles fought back his embarrassment for H. L. Hix, who had died in a house without a master suite: no walk-in closet, no master bath with his-and-hers sinks, no sliding glass door onto a deck with a view of the mountains.

Neither Prissy herself nor Kirk Stiles sat, since there were no chairs in the room. He had trouble settling what he should do with his hands. First, he clasped them behind his back, but that seemed too leisurely, so he clasped them in front of himself, thinking that made him look more humble and mournful. It would have been easier if he'd had time to grab a drink: one hand holding a wine glass, the other behind his back, *that* would be the right look at this moment, respectful but not so formal that it would appear artificial.

Priscilla Frederickson did not delay. In a low voice, not a whisper, but hushed enough that only Stiles could hear her, even though the door was not closed, she said, "I know you know how things work in this place." He only nodded, not wanting to project either vanity or false humility. "I need advice. He left so many debts," she complained, "I don't know how I'm supposed to pay them all. I know what office to go to at the University to claim the life insurance benefit, but isn't there something else to do in addition to that? Is there no other source from which I can secure even a little compensation from his death?"

Here was a matter in which truly Kirk Stiles could help, but still it was a relief when he was interrupted in his answer by the student Prissy had hired to take people's coats and serve the punch. She laid a coat atop the heap, and looked expectantly at Prissy, indicating that the guests seemed ready for the service to begin. Indeed, it was past the hour. Stiles was relieved, because he'd just caught himself gesturing much more animatedly than was decorous on so sober an occasion. "To be continued," Prissy said, and returned to the main room, with Stiles following, an appropriate distance behind.

decease [From the Latin *decedere*, to go away, itself formed by adding the prefix *de-* to *cedere*, to go, the same root that supplies English with *concession, intercessory, secede*, and so on.] To depart from life. Which occurs with such inevitability that one of the early Bury Wills, from 1463, concedes: "As God disposith for me to dissese."

H. L. Hix here seconds that will's concession, though with "God" as a figure (interchangeable with Fate, Providence, Nature, Necessity…) for whatever it is that "disposith," itself a figure that gives the agency as if behind it were an agent, behind any disposal the Undisposed Disposer. The "dissese," though, deceases from this pattern of figuration: even if there is *only* figure, "dissese" figures as the figure to end all figure.

·

Drive your cart and your plow over the bones of H. L. Hix.

·

A log that can smolder though nothing else burns with it, is not part of the fire.

• • •

H. L. Hix's life had been utterly ordinary, and therefore horrifying.

He'd fallen ill late in his fifties, an age at which he arrived as a professor of a long-dead academic discipline at a university wholly hollowed out by hypocrisy in a sparsely-populated state that no one in Brooklyn could point to on a map, in a town big enough for a Walmart but not for a Whole Foods, a town with plenty of options for deep-dish pepperoni delivered to your door but no place to go for a ramekin of saag paneer.

He'd understood himself as his family's black sheep, just as everyone else thinks themselves their family's black sheep. He and his two sisters, one a year older than him and one a year younger, had been born to a father from a patriarchal family and a mother from a matriarchal one. If ever anyone's childhood and youth merited the description "unremarkable," H. L. Hix's had. His memories were few and fragmentary, not because they'd been repressed but because they hadn't needed to be. What few things he could recollect were inflected not by trauma but by triviality.

He remembered into adulthood, for instance, one sister as a kindergartener barfing through a banister of the split-level their cash-strapped parents were renting, spewing spaghetti and canned corn from the shag-carpeted upper level onto the linoleumed lower, and the other sister in that same house crying after an earthquake shook from the wall her school-project rooster drawn with a variety of dried beans glued to a nine-by-nine square of layerboard. He remembered the

Christmas those sisters got matching mittens in their stockings, and he got gloves. He remembered the clacking of keys and the emphatic ding of the carriage return as his mother typed carbon-papered dissertations into the night to make ends meet. He remembered the affectless whap whap whap the school building's rust-red brick façade echoed back to his birthday-gift off-brand dime-store rubber basketball, dribbled against sun-dulled, sneaker-wearied blacktop.

He remembered the textured tin that covered the aft side of seatbacks on the school bus, and the yellow piping at the border seams of the green vinyl seats. He remembered the shallow timbre of melmac against formica, olive green plate placed onto harvest gold countertop. He remembered the knocking of the dust-toupéed radiator, mornings in his second-grade classroom, and the rattling of his sill-rotted bedroom window, gusty nights that same winter. He remembered one teacher, Mrs. Wargel, pointing on the pull-down map to a state she called *Massatooshuss*, and another, Mrs. Ridout, rolling chalk back and forth between her hands, clicking it against her wedding ring, tick, tick, tick. He remembered the penny scotch-taped, wheat side up, to the ivory-colored molded-plastic arm of the suitcase record player that thirty-three his father's Merle Haggard and his mother's Andy Williams, mapping Moon River mornings after breakfast and Muskogee, Oklahoma evenings after work. He remembered singing along to "You're So Vain" at the roller rink, too dizzied by the flashing lights and tight turns to wonder what the word "gavotte" might mean. He remembered watching cliff diving in rabbit-eared black-and-white, Saturday afternoons on Wide World of Sports, and later, weekday evenings, Jacques Cousteau specials on a 25" Zenith color console. He remembered the drip of sticky purple syrup from a quickly soggy pointed paper cup on sno-cone day, once each summer at Vacation Bible School.

Maybe it would have been made easier for someone else, but for H. L. Hix acceptance of mortality was made harder by the recognition that his life had been composed of transitories, inconsequentials, ephemera. Nothing that had mattered most to him had mattered much to anyone else, and nothing that had mattered to him then still mattered to him now. Far from finding it reassuring that he could bring back to mind a few things that had passed, he found it distressing that everything he could remember *had* passed away. In what sense, he worried, was the rememberer present, if the remembered was not?

•

If H. L. Hix's childhood had been unremarkable, his student years had been even more so. Freshman year at a sturdy state university in a bustling metropolis, the other three at a tiny, backward denominational college in a smaller, slower city nearer home. The usual change of major, in his case from engineering (once he figured out it wouldn't lead to the career he'd been counting on, making pencil drawings of imagined race cars) to English and philosophy. He'd been an RA in the dorm his last three years, not because he had impressive leadership qualities or refined social skills but simply to help pay his way. Those were the days when, with a decent scholarship and a part-time job, one could put oneself through college without a house-note-size debt at the end. No coed dorms at that staid church college, so for three years he'd toted his shampoo down the hall to and from the shower, with a towel wrapped around his waist, and peed under a magic-markered line, at eye level on the wall above the urinal, labeled with the inscription, "If you can piss above this line, the fire department wants YOU!"

He'd taken freshman comp with a gray-ponytailed Woodstock leftover who leaned back in his chair and rested his dingy wallabees on the desk at the front of the room, Latin with a professor whose thick glasses were always lotion-smudged because she took them on and off by the lenses, philosophy with a professor whose tic of grasping his head at points of perplexity in lecture left his bald scalp chalk-dusted by the end of each class session, history in an 8 o'clock class with a Michelin Man who locked the classroom door precisely at the hour so late arrivals couldn't enter, then shouted *Go away!* at any latecomer with the temerity to knock, and lit survey with a professor who found occasion in every class to cite, in her quavery voice, always the same assurances, from Browning's Pippa and Julian of Norwich. He'd have had brightly-colored cords to complement his gown at graduation, if there'd been a category for media cum laude.

•

His career had followed the trajectory of ordinariness on which his childhood and his student years had launched him. He'd taught at a small private college for fifteen years, and at a mid-sized public university for another fifteen. He'd taught mostly intros and surveys, because it was mostly intros and surveys that were taught, of what he taught where he taught. Neither place (no place) needed or wanted more than a token of what he taught. To keep his job and get promoted, the rules said he had to write a book about another book, so he did. He took his turn as chair, because where he worked you took turns chairing, and he did a term as dean because his older colleagues knew not to. His grades always followed a bell curve, and his student evaluations were good enough. He held office hours unfailingly; the students who needed to see him didn't visit, and the students who didn't need to, did. At one job he had lived far enough from campus that he had to drive, but at the other he could walk or bike.

H. L. Hix had chosen a career as a professor because his professors when he was a student had seemed to him so understanding, so wise. His career as a professor had shown him that it was the situation alone that had made those people seem so exceptional. His professors had seemed wise to him because they knew a lot that he didn't know about what he'd enrolled in the class to learn. Thirty years of his career had shown him that professors were as wise as people in other professions, but no whit wiser, and that he himself was more or less as wise as the person in line ahead of him at the grocery checkout, but certainly no wiser than the person behind. From leaning so many times against so many jambs of so many office doors, from coloring in the o's and p's and g's on so many amendments and agendas in so many committee meetings in so many semesters, he'd learned that professors were not unusually wise, but were strongly inclined to think themselves so.

·

H. L. Hix's personal life was as ordinary as his career. He lived by himself until he didn't. At a party in a colleague's home one evening, he was looking for a place on the kitchen counter to set down his plastic cup of wine so he could slip out and head home, when he heard in the next room a laugh he hadn't heard before, a laugh that made *him* laugh. He kept his cup, and followed the sound of that laugh to its source,

Priscilla Frederickson. Without interrupting their conversation, she and the two others with whom she was talking shifted slightly, to make just enough room for him to join them. He arrived for the punch line of the joke one person had been telling: "I don't know, but he's got the Pope driving for him!" There went that laugh again. He lingered long enough for there to come a moment when the two of them were standing by themselves. She agreed to meet for coffee one morning the next week.

No one was surprised by what followed, because everyone agreed that H. L. Hix needed an injection of life into his life, and that someone who could pull off the name Prissy was just the person to administer the dose. Coffee one week led to lunch the next. Their knees meeting under the small table led, with a step or two in between, to her moving in. Their taking turns preparing their lunch boxes led to disagreement over fold-top sandwich bags or zipper-seal. *They'll make a great couple* eventually became *that's how they've always been. Like no one I've ever known* turned in time into *I know everything about you* and then into *I thought I knew you.* His having plenty to work through with his therapist led to her having plenty to work through with hers.

H. L. Hix's failures, too, were ordinary. Debt, for instance. H. L. Hix did nothing egregious in regard to money: he didn't have a gambling addiction or keep a collection of vintage Ferraris in a row of climate-controlled garages. Still, all the things you work to be able to have or do become things you go to work to pay for, and H. L. Hix and Prissy sank over time more and more deeply in debt. All their monthly payments would have been within their means: their house note, the leases on their modest cars, their utility bills, all the little things like streaming services. But they thought they'd learn to play piano, so they bought a six-foot baby grand, and it took significantly longer to pay it off than their weekly lessons lasted. And they liked to travel, to see things while they were young enough to get around easily. So they had their pockets picked at Macchu Picchu, got a gorgeous sunset shot of orange clouds over Angkor Wat, floated low over giraffes and elephants in a hot air balloon at the Maasai Mara, earned their scuba certification on Palau. For which adventures they needed decent luggage and good cameras. They made it a principle only to go somewhere when they found a special deal, but the next great deal always came around before the last one was quite paid for, and seeing one place made it necessary to see two others. Their credit card debt started slowly, and didn't seem like a problem at all until it was much too big a problem to solve. So they *didn't* solve it. They used one credit card to pay off another, and planned when things got out of hand to declare bankruptcy and start fresh. *If they wanted us to pay them off, they shouldn't charge such crazy interest rates*, H. L. Hix would say occasionally to Prissy by way of justification, counting on her to concur.

Even H. L. Hix's tragedies were ordinary. Not six months after doctors told H. L. Hix and Priscilla Frederickson that they could not have children (low sperm count and low motility chief among the several factors), she was pregnant. Not six months after that, they had the nursery decorated with jungle animal wallpaper and furnished with a three-piece nursery set: matching crib, dresser, and glider chair. They ordered a doorplate, hand-painted with the baby's name. Not a month after furnishing the room, they closed it, a miscarriage having rendered it superfluous. Not two years after that, they had someone come in while they rented a place on Lamu, to remodel the nursery into a home office.

•

H. L. Hix had not expected his life to go the way everyone else's life goes, and in that expectation he had been just like everyone else, since no one thinks their life will go the way everyone else's goes, until it has gone that way. Everything that happened in H. L. Hix's life had felt to him unique and exclusive; in this, it was just like everything that happens in everyone else's life.

decline [From the Greek *klinein*, to bend, the source, too, of Lucretius' coinage *clinamen*, the swerve.] The process of sinking from a stronger into a weaker condition; gradual loss of vitality. Charles Aleyn's antique couplet may sound a little creaky, but it's hard to dispute: "When Bodies cease to grow, 'tis the presage / Of a decline to their decrepit Age."

It circulates as a cliché, in sermons and on Facebook posts, the dull question "If you can lose it, was it ever really yours?" Even slightly sharpened, though, into "If you can lose your vitality, was it ever really yours?" it makes a much cleaner cut. As H. L. Hix declined, he had time to mull whether the vitality he was losing had been ever really his.

•

What wobbles on pudgy knees and smooth palms at prime, favors the foot with a cracked heel at sext, and shits his sheets at compline?

•

All animals are transient, but some are more transient than others.

•

All shall be ill, and all shall be ill, and all manner of thing shall be ill.

So sudden and sharp was the pain in his side that H. L. Hix's knees went weak. He barely kept them from buckling. One hand instinctively lurched to the epicenter of the pain. Only later, replaying the incident, would he notice such details as the autonomic correlation of right hand moving to cover right kidney: purpose with no need of conscious intention, the human body attesting to its wonder not merely as its frailty is exposed but in that very exposure. Nothing of the sort, though, had occurred to him during the event, pain having emptied him for that long moment of anything but itself.

As his mind gradually returned, H. L. Hix had to piece things together, because his *experience* of events had not followed the order of their *occurrence*.

First he'd felt that shooting pain. Only then, after the initial blast to his nerves, did he hear the slapping sound of something very hard hitting something very soft, followed by the sharp report and the almost-instant echo from a ricochet. Not until after that had he felt the jolt that passed through shivered machinery into his hands.

In actual order, what had happened was: his lawnmower had kicked up a stone that, deflected off the siding of his house, struck him just below his ribs. Though large, the stone was so smooth that it had not torn the T-shirt (from a 10K he'd lumbered through twenty years before) that H. L. Hix was wearing loosely, not tucked into the scraggly homemade cut-offs he wore only for yard work because the right leg was a little longer than the left, and there was a faded patch, practically a hole, near each back pocket where, before they'd been "retired" as jeans, his bicycle saddle had worn them thin.

He stared at the stone, there at his feet, and already registered as irony its having just the size and shape of a kidney. He couldn't hear himself over the metallic clatter of his beat-up Briggs & Stratton, now even noisier than before, because a little farther out of balance for having struck so large a stone, but still H. L. Hix said out loud the absurd sentence that had entered his mind involuntarily: "You're kidneying me." Even as it passed his lips, he was glad that neither he himself nor anyone else could hear his words over the noise of the mower. It was a stupid thing to think, and an even stupider thing to say, but for H. L. Hix the moment of receiving a mortal blow occasioned neither epiphany nor eloquence.

•

He had been mowing his driveway when the fatal incident occurred.

H. L. Hix lived in a century-old railroad house on a corner lot in Laramie, Wyoming, in "the tree area," so called because Laramie's harsh climate (its combination of high altitude, unremitting aridity, and extreme cold) proves no less inhospitable to trees than it does to humans, so only in the older neighborhoods around downtown and the university has planting and tending had time to nurture sources of shade. Mostly cottonwood and Russian olive, some poplar and bur oak, here and there an aspen. For all its testing of trees, though, Laramie's climate does not in the least discourage dandelions, with which H. L. Hix's badly-out-of-level gravel drive was densely overgrown. He'd tried for a year or two to keep the drive clear, spending hours on his knees wielding a v-notch hand weeder, but he'd forfeited that losing fight.

The dandelion cover accounted for the mowing that ultimately deprived H. L. Hix of anything beyond banality to blame for his death. Roof replacement after a recent summer's sudden hailstorm meant that the house had umber shingles almost as fresh as its sea-green paint was weary. The other houses facing 6th Street on his block backed up to an unpaved alley, but his, because it occupied a corner half lot, had no alley access. Instead of a back yard bounded by a detached garage that faced the alley, like all his neighbors' houses had, H. L. Hix's house (the oldest on the block, built before horseless carriages and stop signs and interstate highways) had, pushed right up against it, what had been built as a barn, before its much later conversion into a garage. Now, after further renovation, this small outbuilding functioned as a shed instead of a garage, housing the lawnmower and the aluminum extension ladder rather than covering a car. Housing, too, pyramidded paint cans with drip-stained labels and their lids tamped tight using a screwdriver handle for a hammer, a leaf rake with two of its red tin tines bent away from the otherwise symmetrical fan, a yellow molded-plastic toolbox cluttered with the crescent wrenches and pliers that H. L. Hix had never learned to be handy with. An empty 12-gallon gray plastic snap-lid storage bin inside a 20-gallon clear plastic bin. A small olive-green rough-canvas duffel bag, zipped inside a larger matching duffel bag that hung by its shoulder strap from a 16-penny striker nail. A bucket with a puckered lip for pouring, and a half-circle metal handle with a plastic-tube grip; sundry spades and pruning shears; an oscillating sprinkler; an electric drill with a badly crimped and much too short cord. Two six-foot indoor extension cords, one white, one brown, jumbled in a plastic grocery bag hung from the knob of a drawer, and a fifty-foot outdoor extension cord with bright orange insulation, loosely looped, lying on a shelf. At first, H. L. Hix had set out mousetraps, but soon he conceded that contest, too. In place of eliminating mice, he determined not to notice their droppings.

Instead of opening onto the rutted, untrafficked back alley, the shed faced Sheridan, a through street. Backing out into Sheridan traffic was too much trouble and would be just *asking* for a wreck, so it was easier to park on 6th Street in front of the house than to use the driveway. April hail would pock the Hyundai, parked in either place.

With no Firestones fretting them, dandelions flourished.

•

On the day of the mowing accident, little knowing what trouble he was inviting, H. L. Hix had gone for gas. High desert climate meant his yard (that day as every day) was a shambles, but offered in compensation that what skimpy lawn there was didn't often need mowing. A couple of times in late spring, while snowmelt still moistened the soil, but not at all after that, once the dirt dried out in the short, rainless summer. Still, his gas can was empty that day, and the filling station stood just far enough off to make walking too much trouble. Getting to the station would be fine, a nice five minutes in the fresh cool morning air, but lugging the full two-gallon can back even those few blocks wasn't worth it, so he'd driven. First he topped off his car, then filled the yellow-and-red gas can. He liked the slight difference in the rising pitch with which each signalled it was nearly full. He liked their contrasting timbres: car a muffled gurgle, can a buffered hiss. The dust that, because he parked on the street instead of in a garage, always layered his car exempted no part of its surface, so he took the occasion of the fill-up to squeegee clean his windshield, adding, even though he almost never drove at night, one swipe for each headlight.

Mowing had been going well until the kicked-up rock. He'd taken care to keep the mower clear of the hollyhocks that had seeded themselves along the head-high cedar privacy fence separating his driveway from the neighbors' yard. Those neighbors, a hetero couple, twenty-somethings sopped with the soothing sense of entitlement that permits one to *feel* goodwill toward others while *doing* them harm, had backed their four-door F-150 (without apology, without seeming even to notice) over a prior stand of hollyhocks when, soon after buying the house, they'd replaced the previous fence, so H. L. Hix had been nurturing the new volunteers.

In the moment preceding the accident, the mower was at its fastest. It rattled and clanged, not from age per se (old though it was) but from neglect, from never having been maintained beyond occasionally confirming that its oil level had not fallen below the dipstick's fill line. H. L. Hix had never achieved the level of mechanical prowess that would enable him to replace the mower's plug and filter, but topping off its oil was within his narrow range of competence. It didn't smoke as badly as, from its rattle, you'd expect, but over the course of mowing even the small half-lot, the mower slowed and slowed until it was hardly going at all, a pattern that H. L. Hix tried *not* to interpret as a fable elucidating his own life. As usual, though, because the shed in which the lawnmower was stored opened onto the driveway, H. L. Hix had started there, so as he approached the fateful stone, his mower's noisy four-stroke, whatever tendency it might have to falter later, was at its strongest then.

So stunned had H. L. Hix been by the rock-kick to his kidney that he'd stood for quite some time, staring down at the assailant stone, right hand hard to his side, left hand securing the safety bar that kept the mower's motor going. Slowly the pain began its transformation into ache, and eventually H. L. Hix looked up, looked around, and (his capacity for decision now restored) released the bail switch that let the stertorous mower stutter down to silence.

He gave the sounds that had been mower-buried time to resurface: passing cars, sparrow chatter. He gave his body time to adjust to its new condition, and to begin its protest. He told himself the pain was not so intense that he couldn't continue to push the mower, but he decided against finishing the lawn, because he *didn't* think he could restart the pull-start mower, and he wasn't willing to try.

The welt raised by the stone's impact went down after just a day or two, but the residual bruise was big (his whole right side, armpit to waist) and ugly (a gruesome saffron-splotched, pitch-tinged eggplant purple), and tender to the touch. Slowly, though, for all its initial prominence, the bruise shrunk, and eventually it disappeared altogether. The stone hadn't broken any ribs, so after several days of painful breathing and a few nights past that of difficulty sleeping, there seemed to be no lingering physical effects, or at least nothing to indicate that permanent damage had occurred. H. L. Hix meant to look up whether it was possible for injured ribs to go unbroken because they were hit too *hard* rather than too softly, but he never got around to it. He consoled himself with the cliché "No harm, no foul," and soon put the mowing incident behind him.

delible [From the Latin *delebilis*, susceptible to being blotted out.] Liable to be deleted or effaced. A condition, Richard Bentley in his *Eight Sermons* cautions, that we humans all of us suffer, leaving after death only "the deleble stains of departed souls."

Contemporary usage employs only the negative form, *indelible*, as when Plath in her fever rehearses "The indelible smell // Of a snuffed candle," but the stains from H. L. Hix's vagrant soul, always dark, and often also foul, didn't even wait for its departure before proving themselves delible.

•

Dead, H. L. Hix revenges not injuries.

•

A tree whose branches tangle through each other though no other branches tangle with them, is not part of the forest.

•

All shall be stale, and all shall be stale, and all manner of thing shall be stale.

H. L. Hix occasionally groused about a sour taste in his mouth and a slight stitch in his right side, but though each was an ongoing annoyance, both were low-grade, neither of them bad enough to make much fuss about or go to the doctor over.

Still, the persistence and the incremental escalation of those initially minor symptoms made H. L. Hix even more temperamental than he had been before, as if he were *trying* now to justify Prissy's constantly complaining that he constantly complained. Her accusation that he had a bitter disposition, an ill temper that no one other than herself would have put up with for all these years, had more to do with her tendency to exaggerate than with his personality, but it was true that since the injury he started their petty quarrels more often than she did, and much more often than he had before.

They could not sit down to dinner, for instance, without his finding something over which to pick a pointless fight. Did she have to put the salad, he would snark, on the same plate as the main course? Did she have to drown the salad in dressing, he would carp one night, and was she trying to save money by skimping on dressing, the next. Why did she insist on setting out sea salt in that finicky crystal finger bowl instead of serving normal salt from a normal shaker like normal people used? Why the fussy cloth napkins that had to be repeatedly laundered, instead of more convenient paper napkins they could just pitch? Leftovers again? It wasn't that he cared about the things he complained about, or that he disliked anything Prissy had done, or that he liked arguing. It was as if a living entity (our name is *Angelfear*, for we are both) had taken up residence inside him, as if now it were using his body, his mouth, to speak what it wanted to say, whenever it wanted. As if "I'm not myself today" were *literally* true of H. L. Hix, and true of him *every* day. He really *wasn't* himself, and never had been.

At first Prissy defended herself. A separate salad plate only makes more dishes. A little extra dressing masks how sad the lettuce was this week at Safeway, a little less dressing cuts out a lot of calories and fat. Sea salt still has extra nutrients, magnesium for instance, that have been bleached out of table salt. Haven't we been trying to cut down on what we throw away? Soon, though, she saw that her rational responses were not a way to end his irrational complaints. She decided not to let herself be provoked, insisting to herself, "I simply won't be drawn into the bickering." She congratulated herself for taking the high road in this way, but also felt sorry for herself because it was always she who *had* to take the high road. She saw that the best moments of her being with H. L. Hix hadn't been exactly blissful even when they'd been occurring, and now they all were lost to a distant, unrecoverable past. She saw that her relationship with him had been the biggest mistake of her life, the one that tainted everything else.

Priscilla Frederickson had always been one to want to be the first of a couple to die. She had wanted to be the one grieved, not the one grieving, but not any more: this deterioration in H. L. Hix, this souring of his very soul, changed her mind. He was a dead mouse hidden in the walls, itself out of reach, but sending the stench of its rot through the whole house. He was the algal bloom turning a whole pond toxic, leaving bleached fish corpses matted into clusters cluttering its shore. Now she wished he would die first, and she wished he would die *soon*, to let her recover some semblance of inner peace. She decided he was *acidic*. He's an acid rain, she said to herself, soaking into me through my leaves and roots, flamelessly but inexorably scalding me to death.

•

After one especially ruthless outburst, H. L. Hix, trying to make some excuse for his unwarranted ill temper, had finally admitted to Prissy, as if she hadn't been able to discern the fact on her own, that he'd been feeling unwell. She was still smarting from the insult, so in response to his excuse for it she had snapped back, "And what do we do when we feel ill? Who do we make an appointment to see?" For once, H. L. Hix did not continue the argument, didn't insist on getting in the last word. Only when she said it out loud did he admit to himself what, though he'd been denying it, he well knew: that he was sick and getting sicker, that he was *behaving* badly because he was *feeling* bad, and that it really *was* time for him to see the doctor. He'd always been afraid of doctors, but now he was even *more* afraid of his illness.

His visit to the clinic began with his filling out various forms, each less concerned than the last with his physical health and more with the medical industry's fiscal health. On the form that asked for family medical history, he should have been able to go farther back than in fact he could. His father had died of pneumonia, his mother of natural causes. That much of course he knew, and he wrote it out with confidence, watching the plastic daisy taped atop the ballpoint the receptionist had handed him along with the clipboard, almost able at this moment to read the mirror image of his words as if the flower wrote them in pretended pollen onto air. "Onto thin air," he said to himself in his head, not concerned about misquoting, "and like the baseless fabric of this vision shall dissolve, and leave not a rack behind."

At every remove from his parents, his knowledge of familial health failures grew less secure, more second- or third-hand. There were pacemakers aplenty and stents galore, even a titanium valve or two, but assigning each to its proper corpse was more than H. L. Hix knew how to do. His father's mother had died in her sleep, but not before her dementia had hail-damaged his father's father, whose heart, having had enough, gave out. His mother's father succumbed to a stroke, his mother's mother to old-fashioned old age (wallpapered at the very last with UTI-induced hallucinations). His aunts and uncles expanded the repertoire. On one side, diabetes, heart attack, sideswipe by a double-trailer semi on a rain-slick interstate; on the other, overdose, anorexia, hepatitis, a Browning to the brain. Farther afield (second cousins and such distant kin) there were cancers of all kinds: lung cancer, liver cancer, leukemia, lymphoma, cancer of the colon, the skin, the breast, the soft palate, you name it. Not a floating kidney in sight, but not much need for one, not with cancers so plentiful and various, available to any organ or limb. Farther back (great grandparents, great uncles and aunts, great-greats of all sorts) there'd been dysentery, tetanus, and croup. Yellow fever, scarlet fever, a fever for nearly every crayon color. There'd been a railroad bridge collapse, some enemy artillery in various wars for freedom, on one occasion gangrene, more than once cirrhosis of the liver. Miscarriages, stillbirths, neonatal hyperbilirubinemia. Rubella, polio, mumps, consumption, whooping cough. Each event or condition more than enough.

As a kid whose clumsiness could sometimes overcome his considerable fraidy-cat caution, he'd occasionally been taken to emergency rooms. In those days, in those places, nurses had worn white bobby-pinned red-pinstripe-bordered cardboard caps (folded to look like they were upraised wings), white dresses with two pairs of white patch pockets on the front, white stockings, white rubber-soled pumps. Today, in this clinic, the nurse who led him back to the exam room wore dark blue short-sleeved scrubs (with a laminated data-rich ID card clipped to the shirt pocket) and white sneakers. This nurse had pronounced H. L. Hix's name as a question to the waiting room, then led him down the hall, at a brisker pace, H. L. Hix thought, than an ailing patient should be expected to match, without looking back to see if he was keeping up. Had flipped out one of the saturated-color plastic signal flags from the set attached to the wall by the door to the room, shown him in, taken his temperature and pulse rate and blood pressure, shone a small but quite bright light into his eyes and ears and his tongue-depressored mouth, declared (in a tone more perfunctory than calm and assuring) that the doctor would arrive soon, and left him there without another word.

•

Priscilla Frederickson and H. L. Hix had argued over whether she would or would not go with him to the clinic, but he had won the argument, so he was by himself now as he waited for the doctor. While he'd been in the waiting room, he'd thought of six-year-old Elizabeth Bishop reading the *National Geographic,* rather than himself picking up the nerve-worn *Men's Health* offered him on the smoked-glass surface of the pressed-board-framed coffee table with its faux-walnut-grained vinyl veneer. He didn't know, though, of any poems about examination rooms to help distract him, so he looked at the clear plastic wall rack of trifold leaflets: YOUR REPRODUCTIVE HEALTH in all caps under a photo of a smiling, very pregnant black woman; STROKE? ACT F.A.S.T. in bold over four captioned line drawings of an increasingly puzzled-looking white-haired white man; and so on. He imagined the doctor ending his appointment by reaching for a pamphlet to hand him along with a scribbled prescription. RE-INFLATE YOUR COLLAPSING KIDNEY, it would say, with a picture of him on the front, one hand on the lawnmower handle, one holding his side, looking more befuddled than hurt.

•

The doctor entered as abruptly as the nurse had left, as if the departing nurse had handed off an indifference baton to the arriving doctor. She opened the door, entered the room, closed the door, rolled the castered stool into position, and sat, all without making eye contact with H. L. Hix or in any way acknowledging his presence, but instead looking with deeply-furrowed brow at the tablet in her left hand. H. L. Hix missed the fliptop metal clipboards from the old days. Their materiality, their *solidity*, and even their sound, had lent authority to the bearer, making it appear as though the doctor were calmly recording some salient portion from a rich store of accrued practical wisdom, not cluelessly checking to see what Google offered up for the keywords of the mysterious symptoms. The office area behind the receptionists in the waiting room had one whole wall of paper files. Floor-to-ceiling shelves filled with thousands of manila folders filed vertically, each with a color-coded tab. Apparently they served now, though, only for ambience, a signal to worried waiting patients that they were under the watchful eye of Medicine, one reassurance to be seconded soon by the symbolic stethoscope looped over the collar of a confidently left-unbuttoned lab coat.

The doctor had dark features and an ample build that recalled to H. L. Hix's mind the bemused self-description a favorite cousin of his often gave: "I'm built for comfort, not for speed."

"Not feeling well?" the doctor asked, without introducing herself, and looking up only after asking the question. It was true his name was on her tablet, and hers was pinned to her lapel, so he had to admit to himself that introduction would be an idle formality.

H. L. Hix began to describe the symptoms, but he made less and less sense, even to himself, the longer he spoke. The doctor did not look in his eyes while he was speaking, or give any appearance of listening, but busied herself reiterating the symbolic gestures (take his blood pressure, look in his ears…) that the nurse had performed already. He tried to describe the taste in his mouth, the lingering ache in his side. He told about the stone, sort of: he changed it to bumping into a door knob because the lawnmower in the driveway story was too embarrassing. The connection sounded silly, though, with or without the fib. Why would a bump to his side create a sour taste in his mouth? He must sound to the doctor like yet another ignorant hypochondriac patient postulating some folk-medicine cause for his psychosomatic symptoms.

H. L. Hix wanted the answer to one either/or: can my health be restored, or will this condition debilitate me? benign or malignant? will I live or will I die? The doctor evaded this either/or altogether. She spoke only of (and seemed interested only in) a different either/or: neutropenic enterocolitis, or renal papillary necrosis? caecum, or kidney? The doctor didn't deign to address H. L. Hix's irrational fear that this was rapidly-spreading stage-four cancer, a fear she would anyway have waved away: cancer isn't caused by contusion. "No, but can a bruise set cancer loose?" H. L. Hix would still have worried. "Don't be silly," she'd have said impatiently. "You can't get cancer from bumping into things."

In fact, she said, "We'll need to run some tests." Still looking at the pad, now with her head cocked a little. "The nurse will get samples, and the front desk will schedule your next appointment." And so it was. The nurse secured from H. L. Hix a blood sample and a urine sample. The front desk scheduled him for the first of the tests the insurance company would authorize, in the sequence the insurance company mandated, in order to determine what surgery and what pharmaceutical regimen would be most cost-effective.

•

H. L. Hix walked slowly from the clinic to the parking lot, and sat for a few minutes in his car before starting it up and beginning the drive home. He'd heard enough legends about doctors in Laramie to know to go down to Fort Collins for health care, so the return drive gave him an hour to try to register the doctor's withholding any diagnosis. The doctor's overcautious approach — not identifying his illness or outlining a cure, but insisting that tests were needed — implied that for all her medical expertise, she knew nothing more about H. L. Hix's condition than he did. She could confirm what he knew already, that his body was failing, but she couldn't say why. She could confirm that there was a problem, but she couldn't fix it.

287 between Fort Collins, Colorado, and Laramie, Wyoming, is a dangerous stretch of road: it connects two university towns, so it hosts in disproportionate numbers drunk nineteen-year-olds double-daring one another; it goes through mountains, so it has blind curves and narrow bridges; it's two-lane most of the way, but hilly and heavily trafficked by trucks, so drivers get impatient and try to pass even when there's not enough room; it runs north-south and is open to the west, so the crosswinds are strong; it's at elevation, so snow blows across the road and glazes it with black ice seven months of the year. It's dangerous, but it's beautiful: rock formations that look lunar; glacial rubble only bristlecones brave; homemade *No Hunting* signs in white paint on tires hung over fenceposts; sunrise over one line of ridges, sunset over another. On this drive, though, to H. L. Hix, on this day, everything looked brown and dry, sunburnt scrub on open stretches no less than bare rock rising from it. The landscape looked the way he felt.

When he arrived home, he began to tell Prissy about the clinic visit and the doctor's indecisive diagnosis, but her phone rang and, glancing down at it, she signaled "one minute" with the forefinger of her free hand. She angled her head enough to open a gap between hair and ear, put the phone to that now exposed ear, said "Yes?" into the phone, and left the room.

H. L. Hix sighed, and said out loud to himself, "Maybe it's not a big deal." Maybe, his monologue continued, though after that first sentence only in his head, there's nothing to worry about. If it had been something really bad, the doctor would have known, and would have said. If it was going to kill me, I wouldn't *need* tests.

It didn't make much sense to H. L. Hix that the doctor *had* prescribed three different medications, when she *hadn't* identified what was wrong. She's just getting a kickback from the drug company, he told himself. But he took them anyway. He bought a plastic weekly pill dispenser when he picked up the prescriptions at the drive-through window of the pharmacy. A *weakly* pill dispenser, he thought to himself while he waited for the clerk to run his credit card.

His taking medications that hadn't been explained to him, and the purpose of which he didn't understand, was obedience, but his attention to matters of health became almost an obsession. He tracked his own physical condition: Did I feel better this morning when I woke than I felt last night when I went to bed, or worse? Better when I woke this morning than when I woke yesterday morning, or worse? Would I call the ache in my kidney at this moment a 6 or a 7? Is that a prickling in my feet or toes, or just a tingling? Is the sharper but more intermittent pain in my finger joints connected to the duller but more constant ache in my side? Why have my finger joints begun to "catch" sometimes instead of moving smoothly? He began to haunt medical websites, sometimes beginning by keying in combinations of his symptoms into a search engine and clicking on the candidate afflictions it offered up. Other times he went straight to a familiar site: the Mayo Clinic, the National Health Service, webmd, healthline. He started listening in on conversations about people's health complaints, instead of ignoring them as he always had before. The doctor had instructed him to drink more water, so he did, and to get more sleep, so he started going to bed an hour earlier and ordered a contour pillow from a bedding store on line.

The pain in his side did not diminish; it even increased. Still, H. L. Hix insisted to himself that he was getting better. This must be what they mean by the aches and pains of age, he decided. I've always been healthy, and that hasn't stopped, but I'm well into my fifties and I'll have to make a few concessions here and there. It's all normal, nothing to worry about. This worked, and he believed this explanation he gave himself, until he "hit a snag" of any sort, however small, even the most trivial impediment: the lid on the orange juice didn't hold its seal, so when he shook the bottle to stir the juice enough leaked out to get his fingers sticky; the zipper handle on his favorite fleece vest came off; the post office returned a parcel for extra postage, even though he'd paid what the damned machine had told him to. Such moments, which in the past would have been minor, brief frustrations, quickly forgotten, now made him furious, and he couldn't let them go. It only added to his anger, that he was behaving in his illness just the way pop psychology said everyone behaved.

demise [From Old French *desmettre*, to dismiss or (reflexively) to resign.] Death, decease. By transference from a prior technical meaning in law: the conveyance of an estate by will or lease. Already thus transferred, though, as early as 1754, when Richardson, in his *History of Sir Charles Grandison*, has one character report of another that "Her father's considerable estate, on his demise, went with the name."

This conveyance, in its own way a will, would have invited replacing "death" with "demise" more often (replacing it even in the title) if H. L. Hix's estate *or* his name had been more considerable.

·

What crawls on shag carpet in the morning, stumbles on tree-root-troubled sidewalks at noon, and drools onto daily-laundered-and-tumble-dried hospital-white cotton-polyester pillowcases at dusk?

·

All animals are fleeting, but some are more fleeting than others.

·

All shall be null, and all shall be null, and all manner of thing shall be null.

·

… shall dissolve and, like this insubstantial pageant faded, leave not a shoeboxful of washed-out Walmart-printed vacation photos behind.

• • •

H. L. Hix knew that he was dying. Presented with the question "Are you dying?" on a true/false quiz, he'd have correctly circled the T. But it didn't make sense. He knew it, yes, no problem acing that quiz, but he couldn't *understand* it. He knew it the way he knew the earth's circumference was 25,000 miles, not the way he knew a cold front was blowing in. He knew it the way he knew he was spinning very fast around the earth's axis even though it *felt* like he was standing still.

The problem wasn't lack of information, and it wasn't failure of logic. H. L. Hix had been shown the standard syllogism in one from the string of listless lectures that faux-pearl-necklaced the sophomore logic section he'd been mistakenly placed in during freshman year, but he'd been shown it only as an evidence that any generality is subject to other generalities in ways that make for elegant and intricate patterns, not shown it as a salience that pointed, even potentially, to him in particular, or pointed to anything particular to him. *Socrates is a human. All humans are mortal. Therefore, Socrates is mortal.* Makes sense, yes. Still (the lecturer's sideburned and combovered indifference instructed), don't make too much of it, don't make it something it's not. No blood in that turnip, no water in that stone.

H. L. Hix saw the lecturer's indifference, which came from knowing something too well, and raised it with an indifference of his own, which came from knowing nothing at all. Socrates was an abstract human, a name, a syllogism-filler, a representative of abstract humanity, and thus unlike living, breathing, able-to-see-himself-in-a-mirror H. L. Hix who had to shave his patchy stubble every day and trim his fungus-bloated toenails once a month. Socrates did not have a thin scar hidden by his left eyebrow, from having fallen as a toddler into the corner of a coffee table. Socrates had never waited on the grade behind the shabby two-bedroom his parents rented, to wave at the conductor of a passing freight train's caboose. Socrates had never riveted the handle slightly askew on the sheet-steel dustpan he was made to make for his mother in ninth-grade metal shop. Socrates had never been pushed to play dodge-ball in his school-colors poly-cotton gym shorts in P.E. class, or chosen to play freeze-tag at recess in his knee-patched jeans, cuffed above knock-off converse. Socrates had never panicked in swimming lessons, and had to be pulled from the pool. Socrates had never touched his hand to his nose to smell on it the bluegill he'd just been taught to scale and gut. (Start from the head when you take hold to remove the hook or, later, to pull it from the stringer to clean, so you don't get barbed.) Socrates had never pushed his plastic tray, molded with a surface pattern of fake basket-weave, along the kid-high cafeteria line in elementary school, and drunk milk straight from the fold-out mouth of the 8-oz. coated-cardboard carton. Socrates had never made "pksh, pksh" sounds in his throat while he pointed the rifle-readied inch-high plastic soldier he held between the thumb and forefinger of his right hand at the equally tiny, equally inanimate soldier he held in the same way in his left.

Steer around a roadkill deer, sure, it's big enough to dent your car, but no need to swerve for a tractor-trailer-flattened raccoon corpse that won't do any damage. Socrates was *supposed* to die, that's the point. Socrates never had to take his laundry basket to the line of washers and dryers in the basement of the dorm, never had to choose what shirt to wear to class today, never had to figure out what to do about this broken shoelace. Socrates names whatever demonstrates the admonition *Don't be a dumbshit*, whatever proves the proverb *Homo homini anus.*

Now, though, the syllogism H. L. Hix had been shown so long ago had an altogether different attitude. It didn't just nonchalantly point at him, it stared him down, it put its index finger hard to his sternum and pushed, made him step, even stumble, backward, groping for balance. *Socrates is a human*, it now insisted. *All humans are mortal*, it sneered. *Therefore, H. L. Hix is dying.*

Always before, he had been able to dismiss the mortal Socrates. If I were going to die, he assured himself precisely by *not* thinking it, I would *feel* it. His illness, unwilling to join in the ruse, now deprived him of that assurance. He tried to restore the comforting denial with occasional bursts of attention to his work and with little gifts for Prissy from the antique shop, but he had no success.

Once he even went out and stood in the driveway, exactly where the accident had occurred, thinking that by doing so he could with little coos and soft kissing sounds call his old self back. There were the square plastic bins he rolled out to the street once a week for pick-up, one with a black lid, for trash, and one with a blue lid, for recycling. There was a dark green plastic compost bin, a waist-high half cone with a lid that froze shut in the winter, and over the opening at its base only a flap that the raccoons had bent back. There was the small but visible dent the deflected stone had left in the siding. He could kneel down now and touch the dent if he wanted. Nowhere to be seen, though, was any wholly-unlike-mortal-Socrates self for H. L. Hix to embrace.

•

H. L. Hix could *see* that he was dying, but could not *think* so.

He felt the labor and ache of even simplest movements, actions that not long ago he'd have undertaken with ease and pleasure, and without a thought. Always before, to rise from a chair, for example, had been so effortless, so natural, that he hadn't even noticed it, but now it demanded concentration and exertion. He had to scoot up to the edge of the seat first, then lean forward a little to gain momentum, and he had to use his arms as well as his legs to push himself upright. Even that little bit of pressure added sparks of pain to the smoldering low-grade ache in his knees and hips, his wrists and shoulders.

He saw, on limbs from which the muscles had wasted down, the loose and wrinkled skin not gently curving like wet corrugation, but shriveling like spent shrink wrap, and he saw that same skin's discoloration, from flush with sun-stirred melanin down to its present pallid mucoid hue, from lightly freckle-stippled all the way to heavily liver-spot-spattered. He heard Patsy Cline in his head, but said out loud to her in reply, "I'm not falling to pieces. That would be easy and quick, even pretty. I'm wasting away. It's arduous and slow and ugly, and it smells vile." H. L. Hix had never been beautiful, he well knew, but he told himself he had always stayed fit. His muscles had never been large or shapely, but at least he had kept them toned. He had never stirred tall stacks of iron plates on a weight machine at the gym, but he'd dutifully done his daily routine with sand-filled plastic ten-pound discount-store dumbbells at home. At no point could he have benched his own weight or turned heads at the beach, but always before he'd been able to walk or bike to work, and able to heave his carry-on into the overhead bin. Now he sat, a burlap sack that seed by seed the barn mice were depleting, sagging and sallow and splotched.

He smelled his own ammoniac breath, as if in one lung now a feedlot festered, in the other a stagnant, sewage-clotted slough. He heard his every breath bubble and gurgle through his phlegm-clotted nose and throat. The fetor of his own waste so suffused his room that he himself was never free from it: his sour piss a prick to his sinuses, his rancid shit a sticky film coating his tongue, the roof of his mouth, the back of his throat.

Even his body's incidentals gave evidence that what was on its way was already here. His eyebrows and whiskers were colorless now, brittle and thin. Same with his nails. Hair grew thick from his ears and nose like roots of an undertended philodendron from the drainage holes of a too-tight terra cotta flower pot.

•

H. L. Hix had devoted his whole adult life to making himself a rational animal, but a fist-sized rock kicked up from his dandelion-dense driveway by his tubercular lawnmower had made him, instantly, a dying animal. From Aristotle all the way to Yeats, in a single bound. What had been always distant, the end of the line, was suddenly the next stop. Zero at the bone. Zeno: does one grain of millet make a noise when it falls? Zed's dead, baby, Zed's dead.

departed [From the Latin *dispertire*, to divide.] Gone away, past, bygone. In contemporary usage, most commonly in *the dear departed*, already a familiar phrase by the time of *Mansfield Park*, in which Mrs. Norris hopes "to live so as not to disgrace the memory of the dear departed." This sense, though, only extends the original sense, in which to depart is to divide into parts, to sunder or separate, as in the earliest editions of *The Book of Common Prayer*, which give, not the pledge we know now as "till death do us part," but its more incisive antecedent, "till death us departe."

Death had no difficulty departing H. L. Hix from Priscilla Frederickson, already having departed a prior "us," H. L. Hix's selves, a loose assortment that had not offered much resistance to the sundering.

•

H. L. Hix's death, now proved, was once only imagin'd.

•

A virga that valances the western horizon though no drop from it reaches a parched patch of prairie grass or touches a stretch of soybean, is not part of the rain.

•

All shall be pale, and all shall be pale, and all manner of thing shall be pale.

•

… shall dissolve and, like this insubstantial pageant faded, leave not a line of sole-worn workout shoes behind.

•

Socrates is a human. All humans are mortal. Therefore, H. L. Hix's kidneys are faltering, and his liver function weakens by the day.

. . .

H. L. Hix had been embarrassed always by his bowel movements, and had taken exaggerated, unfailing care to keep them as secret as possible. He never permitted himself use of a public toilet for this purpose: not at his office, not in an airport or restaurant, certainly not during intermission at the theater. Never, either, when invited to dinner at a friend's home or to a party at a colleague's. He even tried to hide his bowel movements from Priscilla Frederickson, always waiting until she was somewhere else in the house, far from the one bathroom. Even during the happier periods of their life together, the pleasure he had taken in travelling with her was compromised by the humiliation of tiny hotel rooms, which precluded his taking a shit in private.

Now, wholly subject to intestines over which in times past he had exerted such strict control, he could not perform his own bowel movements for himself, much less keep them secret. Prissy hired a live-in home health care aide, a young man, Gary Simm, who was studying to become a nurse, and it was he who managed H. L. Hix's excretory functions now.

He went by his full name, Gary Simm, instead of just his given name, because for three years in a row in grade school there'd been another Gary, and teachers in class, like kids on the playground, needed a way to distinguish them. Gary Simm instead of Gary by itself grew so familiar that it stuck. His own mother had begun by then to call him Gary Simm.

Gary Simm was everything H. L. Hix was not: young, healthy, beautiful, athletic, competent, autonomous. Gary

Simm, in short, was full of life. He had good posture, smooth skin, thick hair. His presence therefore offered the shriveling, incontinent H. L. Hix equal parts consternation and consolation. He was unembarrassed by the bedpan, which after each use he removed from the room matter-of-factly, as if it had been a place setting he were carrying off to the dishwasher, or a book he were restoring to its place on a shelf.

On one such occasion, as Gary Simm returned to the room bearing the bedpan he had just emptied and cleaned, H. L. Hix rasped an apology. "Gary Simm," he wheezed, pausing while he closed his eyes to take a breath. He took another breath and opened them, "this must disgust you. I'm sorry. I can't help it."

"Don't apologize," Gary Simm offered in perfect cheerfulness and sincerity, without the slightest affectation. "Everyone gets sick sometimes." His expression seemed neither forced nor smug. "I'm happy I can help. It's what I'm here for."

Gary Simm accompanied these words with a little shrug of his strong, broad shoulders, and followed them with a smile that showed his straight, white teeth. If this brief interaction had occurred as a segment in an animation, rather than as a slice of real life, one front tooth would have sparkled at that moment, accompanied by the *ting* of a tiny bell.

Gary Simm's words, though, did not simply die away. The short conversation stayed with H. L. Hix afterward, spinning off many internal dialogues, progressless repetitions of one another. "So that's what they teach you in nursing school," H. L. Hix would say to himself. "They teach you the same thing you learn in lit survey or philosophy seminar, that people would worry less our surface resemblance to great apes if they recognized our more ultimate resemblance to earthworms. Same number of knuckles as a silverback, but those happenstance appendages that two of us *have* dangle from the gut we all three *are*. In poetry class they teach you to lament being little more than an intestine; in philosophy class they teach you the entailment *I shit, therefore I am*. In nursing school they teach you to deal with the consequences."

·

H. L. Hix had not been bedbound long before he began to wonder what had become of the deathbed cassette tape his paternal grandfather had made. "Deathbed" here was figurative: actually his grandfather had made the tape not lying on his deathbed but sitting on the duct-taped naugahyde overstuffed recliner in the keepsake-cluttered living area of the cramped apartment in the assisted-living community where he and his second wife lived. He'd made the tape while she was out at her pottery-decorating class, painting matching purple iris on a china cup and saucer. And he'd been right about the timing: he'd died within days of making the tape.

H. L. Hix had known better than to ask about details he hadn't been told. Had his grandfather given the tape to his wife before his death, or had he left it atop the battery-powered portable recorder on the TV tray beside the recliner, to be found after his death? Had he wanted it to be played at his funeral? H. L. Hix had received his copy of the tape in the mail, from his parents. How many copies of that confounded cassette had been made? If he was getting one, did that mean copies had been made not only for each of his grandfather's children but for *their* children, too, his grandchildren? What about his great-grandchildren?

The tape started with clicks and rustlings before the gravelly voice gravely began, "Well, dear family, this is just the musings of an old man. I thought I might leave you all a message." On and on it went, for both sides of a 60-minute tape, less and less coherent as it progressed.

•

At the time he received the tape, H. L. Hix had been dismissive. Its righteous tone (H. L. Hix himself had been singled out for scolding, as having gone astray, wandering far from the straight and narrow) and fantastic beliefs (it was insistent about soon walking on streets of gold) seemed to him delusional, and pathetic in their desperation. Now, though, that he himself was pathetic in his own desperation, almost as near his own death as his grandfather had been to his death when he made the tape, H. L. Hix felt much more empathy. He understood the impulse now, as he had not understood it at the time.

He understood now what the tape had performed: while you think you're living, you can believe your story is the story of your life, but once you see you're dying, you realize that your only story is the story of your death. The difference between his grandfather and himself was that his grandfather had a story for his death ready to hand, but H. L. Hix did not.

Even more basic than that, his grandfather had secured *conditions* for a story of his death that H. L. Hix had not secured. His grandfather had an audience, for example, one he could identify, and an audience he could believe *wanted* to hear his story, and was *obligated* to listen to it. He had a *lineage*: children and grandchildren and great grandchildren, not quite so numerous as the stars of the sky and the sands of the sea, but still numerous. He could believe his story was their story, inherently. H. L. Hix had no such audience: no one was *bound* to hear the story of his death, and no one *wanted* to. In telling the story of his death, H. L. Hix might as well have been a spelunker lost in a vast cave system. He could cry out desperately for rescue, or shout curses in angry despair, or plead to Mercy for mercy, or simply wordlessly weep. Didn't matter. No one would hear.

It wasn't only that condition, though. His grandfather also took himself to enjoy *authority*, guaranteed by consonance between his first-person limited point of view and the point of view of The Omniscient Narrator. The story of his death was true, it mattered and had meaning, because it was an episode in The Story. H. L. Hix, by contrast, enjoyed no such authority, experienced no such consonance. All along, The Story had kept *dis*proving H. L. Hix's story of his life, falsifying rather than confirming it, and H. L. Hix's death could only be the final instance of that dissonance between H. L. Hix's story and The Story. If I were to give an account of my own death, H. L. Hix thought to himself, I'd need to write it in close third. I'd need to know my own thoughts, I'd need access to my own interiority, but I've *never* had that, and I can hardly hope to get it now.

•

The ultimate aloneness his illness was enforcing on H. L. Hix was not accompanied by privacy. Even if he'd still had that stupid tape, and a throwback machine on which to play it, he'd have nowhere to go to listen to it, away from Prissy and Gary Simm.

They made sure he knew he had no will of his own, no will not subject to their wills. One afternoon he was awakened from a fitful nap by the two of them pushing next to his bed a hospital bed, the adjustable kind, metal frame, on lockable rubber casters, with railings on each side. He protested, but weakly (he'd been sleeping), and by the time he was alert enough to really argue or resist, they'd moved him onto the new bed and were stripping the sheets from the old. They worked in perfect coordination to remove the old bed from the room and wheel the new bed into the place of the old, without speaking, as if they'd planned and rehearsed their every movement in advance. They didn't respond to his complaints, only glanced at each other periodically, as if to remind one another to keep their pact to ignore his complaints.

deteriorate [From the Latin *deterior*, comparative of **deter-*, itself formed from *de-*, down or away; thus *deterior* meant possessed of relatively more downness or awayness.] To worsen, degenerate, disintegrate. In which process, as Henry Edward Manning has it, each recapitulates all: "there is in the character of the world," he insists, "a law of deterioration, like that which we see in the character of individuals."

A law that H. L. Hix was slow to observe. He saw it first in the downness of other individuals, then in the awayness of the world, but not until a rock-kick to the kidney did he recognize the law of deterioration in himself. Though in all three cases it had been at work the whole time, in plain sight all along.

•

What looks at the floor in the morning, at the horizon at noon, and at the ceiling in the evening?

•

All animals are finite, but some are more finite than others.

•

All shall be small, and all shall be small, and all manner of thing shall be small.

•

… shall dissolve and, like this insubstantial pageant faded, leave not a shallow woven basketful of run-down to-be-recycled batteries behind, not a cupboard of mismatched corporate-logo coffee mugs, upside-down on patterned shelf paper, or a lone coffee mug turned pencil holder, porcupined with brand-stamped ballpoints.

•

Socrates is a human. All humans are mortal. Therefore, H. L. Hix leaks more fluids, from more orifices, more constantly than he once did, each fluid more rancid now than it once was.

• • •

"Gary Simm," H. L. Hix, in his ever-hoarser whisper, asked one day, "would you help me?"

He could never get his temperature quite right; always he was a little too hot or a lot too cold. Now, despite being covered only by the loose ties-down-the-back hospital gown Gary Simm sometimes dressed him in, he was uncomfortably hot and had pushed away the blanket. Even that effort had exhausted him. He was lying on his back, arms at his side, palms up, not turning his head to look at Gary Simm but only moving his eyes.

"I can't find a comfortable position. Please, would you put a pillow under my legs?"

There was a lag now between when H. L. Hix's brain issued words to be spoken and when his mouth actually spoke words it often seemed to have chosen on its own, so while the words were coming out a gauzy thought passed through H. L. Hix's mind, or settled over it, so much mosquito netting. The corpses in old paintings, H. L. Hix thought, or tried to think, don't look comically rigid because the painters lacked the skill for more accurate representation, but because, even without dissecting cadavers in school, they still saw many more corpses than we see now. They knew what corpses look like; it's we who don't. Our dead get taken away immediately, either for cremation or to be prepared in secret, made more "lifelike," which just means made to look as though they were not as rigid as in fact they are. It's not what the old masters painted that's inaccurate; it's how we now see what they painted then that's inaccurate. The fault, dear Brutus, is not in our artists but in ourselves.

The phantom thought was chased away by Gary Simm's reply. "Yes, of course," he said, reaching to pick up a pillow suited to the purpose. In one strong but gentle gesture, he lifted H. L. Hix's legs, positioned the pillow, and settled the brittle, listless twig-legs onto it.

"Thank you."

Gary Simm smiled, wordlessly, and turned back to the fat organic chemistry textbook he was studying.

The relief offered by his altered posture lasted for a little while, but soon enough H. L. Hix called to Gary Simm again. "I'm sorry to keep interrupting you, but can you raise my legs even higher?"

Gary Simm brought a second pillow and placed it under, rather than atop, the first, so as to elevate H. L. Hix's aching legs with as little disturbance as possible. Gary Simm seemed not to have to *think about* or *plan* such courtesies; it was as if he performed them spontaneously, as if they emerged from him like weightless seeds escaping a milkweed pod. H. L. Hix thanked him, but Gary Simm paused, peering at the pillows pensively, as though expecting them to speak. After a moment, he pushed the pillows aside, and positioned himself on the bed in their place, sitting cross-legged, facing the puzzled patient. He lifted H. L. Hix's legs and repositioned them, resting the right ankle on his left shoulder, the left on his right. H. L. Hix closed his eyes and let out a long breath, relaxing into the relief provided by this posture, his frail legs supported by Gary Simm's sculpted torso (suffused with brilliance from inside). To H. L. Hix, relief from pain, however partial, felt like a stay, however temporary, of his death sentence. Gary Simm rested his sturdy hands on H. L. Hix's wasted thighs, periodically kneading them.

•

"Have you never kept pets?" Gary Simm asked one day while they were in what (with mutual satisfaction in having created a lighthearted way to speak about something so intimate) they had come to call the ottoman pose.

"No, the storm that day…," H. L. Hix began to reply, before trailing off. He had slurred his words, pronouncing the *s* in *storm* as if he were saying the German *Sturm*.

Gary Simm had asked because H. L. Hix's eyes had been open, so he had appeared to be awake. His irrelevant answer had shown Gary Simm that in fact H. L. Hix had been (as these days he so often was) "somewhere else," and his answering — actually saying something out loud — had brought him back to the room and the bed.

There was a pause while H. L. Hix gathered himself. "Wait," he said. "Sorry. What? What did you say?"

"I'm sorry I disturbed you," Gary Simm replied. "You were thinking of other things." Another courtesy, to use "thinking" to name H. L. Hix's confused and incoherent mental condition. "I didn't mean to interrupt. I just asked if you had ever kept pets."

"Oh, yes," said H. L. Hix, his pronunciation still blurry but a little clearer now, "always when I was a boy."

Neither spoke for a moment, while H. L. Hix's mind slowly turned itself toward that distant time, now so very far in the past. He was not alert enough to understand that Gary Simm was really asking why he had no pets now, and that simply reporting that Prissy was allergic would be the right answer.

"Dogs," he said. "We had dogs. Always dogs. No cats. Never cats." H. L. Hix's struggle to return to waking consciousness reminded Gary Simm, ironically, of a pull-start lawnmower's halts and hesitations before it levels out to steady rpms. "Sometimes strays. Not long, not inside, we never kept them, never there long." H. L. Hix could not quite cross back over, rejoin himself. The *names* of those dogs, and such words as "littermates," stayed out of reach. He couldn't pull away from that liminal state of awareness that was like being outside in the dark, peering through a window at himself and Gary Simm in a lit interior.

Gary Simm waited patiently while H. L. Hix tried to enter that lit room, and, unable to do so, managed only the one-word question, "You?"

Gary Simm was not one of those talkers who asked his conversation partner questions because he himself wanted to answer them, but neither was he one to decline an invitation to speak. He didn't fail to support H. L. Hix's atrophied legs, and he didn't fail to hold up his end of a conversation.

"In my family it was always cats," he said. "I have a cat now, Sasha. My sister is keeping her for now, while I'm living here with you. She was a stray. My cat I mean, not my sister!" He laughed at himself for having said things in a way that called for that clarification. "Sometimes I call her Wild Thing, because even though she sleeps a lot, when she's *not* sleeping she has little fits of crazy leaping and running. They're very funny. I think she knows it's her nickname and acts out just to hear me laugh and call her that.

"I've always loved cats. Any cat, all cats. They're mysterious, always so fierce, no matter how sweet. I remember once," he said, releasing himself into the memory so that his voice would be continuous, a soothing drone as H. L. Hix faded back into his figure-swallowing fog, "when I was a small child. It's one of my first memories. This was before my father died. He was carrying me on his shoulders. We must have been on a long drive, though I can't think where we'd have been going."

H. L. Hix was back to sleep already. Gary Simm knew his only responsibility now was to keep talking, keep his voice monotonous. It was his job: attend to H. L. Hix's dying body as if it were living, address H. L. Hix's dimmed mind as if it were lit.

"My sister and I must have gotten tired and fussy, because stopping at such places wasn't the sort of thing my parents would normally do, but we were at a zoo. Not a 'real' zoo, the kind they have in big cities, where money and space means at least they can *try* to create settings that give the animals a little room to move, settings that have some small resemblance to the animals' natural habitats. This was one of those really cheesy roadside attractions no doubt started by some dude who never got rid of the baby alligator he'd mail-ordered as a kid, and saw a way to turn an extra buck out back of his gas-station c-store. Probably had a bear out there and a donkey, some such, but — you've been wondering, I know, what this had to do with cats — what I remember is the mountain lion. Its cage wasn't the kind with metal bars: it was long and narrow, with a plexi front, like a giant aquarium, so you could get up really close, of course, but mostly to keep the mountain lion always visible for the paying customers. A clumsily hand-lettered sign warned visitors, *Feirce predator. Do not distrub. Do not tap the glass.*

"Like I say, I was on my father's shoulders. The mountain lion didn't stir: it was on a ledge jutting from the back wall of the cage, lying stretched full-length, totally bored. It seemed not even to notice we were there. But the proprietor — I guess that's who it was, though I remember him as having an unkempt beard, yellow around the mouth, so maybe he was someone the proprietor had minimum-waged into peddling peanuts to toss at the bear — this person, anyway, whoever he was, sidled up to us and said in a bad stage whisper to my dad, *Put the kid down on the ground.* It couldn't have been a threat, but his voice itself sounded threatening to my five-year-old ears. Or at least I remember it *now* as having sounded threatening *then*, maybe because the guy was grinning while he spoke.

"Even as my father was setting me down, the mountain lion's ears perked up, and it raised its head. It looked intently at me, suddenly all attention, instantly transformed from boredom to full alert. The man said to my dad, *Now have your kid run in front of the cage, that way.* My father nodded to me, and as soon as I started to move the mountain lion leapt down from the ledge to chase me. I ran back and forth a couple of times, with the mountain lion after me for those few steps its small cell allowed, making to pounce, glancing off the glass front of the cage, until my father caught me by the wrist and we walked back to the car. My mother was angry. I didn't get then what was going on, but looking back on it now, I can see she must have been feeling that especially intense anger that happens after you've been made to fear. I don't think she spoke the rest of the trip.

"I didn't know the mountain lion would have killed me if not for the cage, I didn't know to think I wasn't the only kid who'd been cajoled into teasing the caged animal, I didn't know to consider whether this might be cruel to the cat itself.

I was a little kid, I thought we were playing, I was doing what I was told by an authority figure to do. I'd never seen a mountain lion except on TV. I thought it was fun."

By this point, H. L. Hix was snoring heavily, so Gary Simm gently put his legs back down on the bed, placed the blanket over them, and returned to studying polysaccharides.

•

When H. L. Hix woke, he was alone in the room. As he lay quietly, he believed for a moment that he could see right through the ceiling to the sky, and right through the stars to the face of God. The bliss, though, was brief. As the ache in his side reasserted itself, he saw that God was scowling. H. L. Hix wept. The tears that, had he been upright, would have flowed from the inner corners of his eyes and run down along his nose to his mouth to mingle their salt with the salt of his snot, because he was lying down flowed from the outer corners of his eyes across his temples into his ears.

He challenged God with the same questions others before him had posed: My God, my God, why hast thou forsaken me? Why do sinners' ways prosper, and why must disappointment all I endeavor end? I cry unto thee, and thou dost not hear me: I stand up, and thou regardest me not.

But H. L. Hix did not expect an answer, or receive one. He let his weeping run its course, and turned his attention inward. If he could not hope to hear the voice of God, he could try at least to hear his own. He thought of the ancient Greek greeting, their equivalent of "How ya doin'?": "Where have you been and where are you going?" But H. L. Hix had been nowhere, he was going nowhere, and he hosted no inner voice to answer his greeting. He tried to look back over where he had been, to enumerate his accomplishments, savor all he had done that would last, but there was nothing to list. His past was parched and barren: the lone and level sands stretched far away. He tried to look forward to where he was going, but he was going nowhere. He was not on a pilgrim's providence-validated progress, but on a patient's insurance-corporation-managed descent from aggressive treatment to palliative care.

double [From the Latin *duplus*, twice as much, but even farther back from the Proto-Indo-European root **pele-*, to fill, and thus cousin to *plenty* and *replete*, *surplus* and *plural*, *fill* and *full*, and all words *poly-*.] A counterpart; an exact copy (of a thing or person). With such ominous connotations as *Light Science for Leisure Hours* registers: "the appearance of a 'double,' or 'fetch,'" Richard A. Proctor there avers, "has ever been held by the learned in ghostly lore to signify approaching death."

H. L. Hix never learned the least ghostly lore, but did feel more *unheimlich* the fewer leisure hours he had left, not because there was by then *also* a double of him, but because there had been ever *only* doubles of him, no original him for the doubles to duplicate. In this collect, those doubles corroborate Adriana Cavarero's claim: "To tell one's own story is to distance oneself from oneself, to make of oneself an other."

•

To create the death of H. L. Hix was the labour of ages.

•

An oxbow shaped by a current though no water now flows through it, is not part of the river.

•

All shall be dull, and all shall be dull, and all manner of thing shall be dull.

•

… shall dissolve and, like this insubstantial pageant faded, leave not a drawerful of heel-weary wool socks and out of-service eyeglasses behind.

•

Socrates is a human. All humans are mortal. Therefore, H. L. Hix no longer hurts only in his fingertips and only when he stays outside a little too long raking leaves on a chilly morning; now he hurts all the time, all over.

$\bullet\ \bullet\ \bullet$

As one more way in which his mind's decline matched his body's, H. L. Hix's dream life, as his health deteriorated, changed its texture from fine sandpaper to coarse hand rasp. Before his illness, he had seldom remembered his dreams upon awakening, but now they asserted themselves often and forcefully. They lingered longer after he woke, especially the ones that had done the waking. They weighed him down, chilled him: waterlogged boot leather.

The dreams themselves were not pretty. If *they* were what was inside him, H. L. Hix told himself, such arrant knaves as he should not be set to crawling between this earth and any heaven. Indeed, should not pretend they haven't crawled already all the way to hell.

One of the first dreams to impose itself as a symptom of his worsening condition featured two small children, first-graders maybe, dressed like girls, white-cotton-blouse-tucked-into-blue-wool-knee-length-skirt school uniforms, schoolgirl ponytails and bangs, but in the dream he knew they both were really boys. They weren't looking at him — in the dream, he wasn't quite himself and wasn't quite *there* — but somehow their faces said they were mean in the ways boys are mean to one another, rather than the ways girls are. Their faces read *burn ants with a magnifying glass* and *pull the wings off of flies*.

The two sinister girl-boys, instead of being seated in small school desks matched to their apparent age, were standing at a lab set-up suited more for college. It was full size, but somehow all its elements were also scaled to their child bodies: rectangular sink, tall gooseneck faucet, smooth black countertop. The girl-boys weren't performing an experiment, though: no bubbling beakers, no petri dishes or test tubes. One demon-child was fingerpainting, the other pasting together a magazine-page collage. No one else was in the room: no other pupils, no teacher. Without warning and without apparent cause, the collaging girl-boy, with a swift stab of her/his rounded-end school scissors, pinned the other's fingerpainting hand to the palmprint turkey it was making on a stretch of butcher paper.

H. L. Hix woke himself with his own crying out, a mixture of the one dream-demon's hideous laughter and the other's hideous scream.

•

As his dreams grew more dramatic and the tedium of the daily routine grew more oppressive, H. L. Hix asked for the ottoman pose more and more often. On one such occasion, the silence between them did not last long after Gary Simm had lifted H. L. Hix's weak ankles onto his own sturdy shoulders. H. L. Hix was exhausted, as usual, and knew he would fade into and out of sleep, but still he uttered his request, saying it out loud this time even though it was understood between them. "Talk to me, Gary Simm. Tell me a story."

What H. L. Hix really *wanted*, of course, was his health. He wanted to be awake again, not in this perpetual dazed half-sleep. He wanted to be able to drive, to walk on his own from the house to the car. He wanted to be able to comb his own hair and clip his own toenails, tie his own shoes, take a piss by himself, standing up, and afterward bend down with two squares of tissue wadded in his own fingers to wipe the toilet rim. He wanted to be able to sneeze without sending little dribbles of shit from his ass. He wanted to be able to eat honey again, and almonds, to go through one whole day without packaged pudding from a plastic cup with a peel-off foil top, to be able to eat *anything* on his own, without assistance and supervision. He wanted to be able to keep his eyes open through a whole paragraph of a book, to be able to remember what he had just read, even to remember what book it was he was reading. He wanted to be alive again, not dying, not already dead.

But Gary Simm could give him nothing of what he really wanted, so H. L. Hix requested what Gary Simm *could* give, that unsatisfying but nevertheless best-available substitute for life, a story.

"I don't know if it really counts as a story," Gary Simm ventured, "but I'll tell you what I was thinking about just now, while I was supposed to be studying. In my Organic Chem class, we've been learning what venoms contain and how they work: neurotoxins, hydrolytic enzymes, and such. Reptiles and amphibians have figured out how to make them, but so have a lot of plants. I spend most of my time in lecture lost, though, and in lab at loose ends. I was a loser in school when I was little, and I'm not a very good student even now. When I prop the textbook open on my lap, I nap or daydream more than I read. I don't understand yet how polypeptides bind to neuronal receptors, but all this thinking all of a sudden about venom did lead me to revisit something that happened when I was a boy.

"We were helping a friend clear back a bunch of badly overgrown brush. The 'we' here was me and my father, but this was when I was a little kid, so of course I wasn't actually any help. I'm sure I'd been brought along only because my mother had errands to run and I was too young to stay at home by myself or with my sister. Who knows where my sister herself was. This was when we lived in Tennessee: it wouldn't have happened here.

"The friend was a friend of my father's, from work. I don't remember his name, but I remember he lived by himself a decent drive out of town, though since then the town has grown so much that his few acres must have been swallowed up long ago. By now, that plot's a subdivision, I'm sure, a bunch of tossed-together houses in four floor plans, evenly spaced, with pasteboard siding tacked to whitewood studs and painted in muted earth tones. What had been, back then, a muddy farm pond, banks pocked with hoofprints and putrid with cowshit, is now a water feature with a fountain at its center. UPS makes a lot of deliveries there from Eddie Bauer and Land's End.

"My father's friend was big, really tall, carrying a belly. (Here, I'll say it in my Anthony-Hopkins-as-Hannibal-Lecter voice: he was a big guy, rrroomy.) One reason I remember him as being so big-boned was his shoes: he wore lace-up boots, but with no laces. He must have had that kind of lower leg — you've seen them — that doesn't taper from wider calf to narrower ankle, but stays all one width from knee to foot, looks like a marble column.

"We hadn't been out there very long before, reaching down to scoop up some leaves, he got bitten by a copperhead. He said it took him a second to figure out what had happened, because the snake only got him with one fang, and he said it felt like something minor, a bee sting or a pinprick, but then he saw the critter slithering away. Funny how well their camouflage works. Neither the color nor the pattern on a copperhead really matches a leaf-litter background, but still you'd never see one sitting there if it didn't move. This was a little-bitty one, my dad's friend said, just a baby. He shrugged the whole thing off at first, said he could barely see the bite, but then his hand started to swell. You could almost *watch* it getting bigger and bigger.

"That's another reason I remember how big he was, the hands. My dad drove the friend's pickup to the hospital, so I had to sit between them. This was a pickup from the old days, a rattletrap, bench seat, column shifter. The friend was laughing, and he showed me his hands: that's the mental image I still carry. His left hand was already big, thick fingers, thick thumb, but the right hand, the one that had been bitten, was *huge*, so ballooned (not just the hand, but by then the wrist and the Popeyed forearm) I was afraid it would burst.

"There's not much else to tell." Here Gary Simm shrugged his shoulders, forgetting for a moment that H. L. Hix's ankles rested on them. Even that small movement, though, felt good to H. L. Hix. Gary Simm continued, "My father's friend didn't die, didn't need his arm amputated, though they kept him in the hospital a good long while (I remember it as *weeks*). I don't think copperhead bites very often kill people, but with any snakebite you have to watch for gangrene.

"My father offered that I could go with him to visit the friend in the hospital, but I didn't, not because I was a rude kid, but because I was a skittish one: afraid of the hospital, afraid of what his hand would look like, afraid I guess of who the man, having been bitten, would have become. As if the snake were a vampire or a zombie, whose bite would have transformed my father's friend into something other than himself.

"Funny, I know, for someone studying to be a nurse to have been afraid that way, but maybe my fear then is behind my vocation now. Maybe my career choice is overcompensation! Maybe I'm here with you to make up for being afraid to go see him."

•

Gary Simm's stories gave relief, but H. L. Hix's illness answered each with a nightmare from which he *needed* relief.

"I'm sorry to wake you," said Gary Simm on one such occasion, "but you were stirring restlessly, as if you were struggling with someone, and you were crying out."

H. L. Hix was only alert enough to mutter "It's OK," as if he were pardoning Gary Simm for some offense, but in fact he was *relieved* to have been awakened. He'd been dreaming of a pair of monstered creatures. One, with the body and the paltry pelt of a possum, its tail, too, like a possum's, long and pink, but carrot-like, thicker than a possum's tail and less flexible, with an armadillo-tough texture to its skin, had burrowed into the foundation of a house that in the dream was H. L. Hix's house. Not burrowed in all the way, just far enough to hide its head: the back half of its body was buried under mounded dirt, from which (through a tidy semicircular opening like a cartoon mouse hole) the tail stuck out, uncovered. Another creature, the first one's inverted double, this one with the head of a possum but with the body of a raccoon, dragged the first creature by the tail from its burrow. The possum-bodied creature, which turned out to have a raccoon's head, tried in its terror to run away, but the larger, faster raccoon-bodied creature pounced on it and killed it by breaking the victim's neck in the predator's jaws. In the dream, the snapping of the small neck had been disproportionately loud, the sound of something much larger, a baseball bat breaking, or even a tree trunk.

H. L. Hix had been grateful to be awakened, because in the dream he had been trying but failing to chase away the raccoon-bodied creature, which was hunched over the possum-bodied creature and, with noisy smacking and slurping sounds, eating its eyes and brain. H. L. Hix had been waving his arms, shouting at the creature and lunging at it, but the creature kept eating, glaring at him as if he were next. His attempts to scare away the creature were futile. He did not frighten the creature; instead, the more frantically he tried to chase it off, the more *he* was frightened by *it*.

dread [From the Old High German *intratan*, to warn against, ultimately from the Proto-Indo-European **ant*, against, source of the English *answer*, and **re-*, to count, source of *reckon*.] Extreme fear, deep awe, oppressive anxiety about future events or conditions. In one of the Trinity Homilies, given as the culmination of a short list of human liabilities: "forgetelnesse, nutelnesse, recheles, shamfestnesse, drede."

The list of H. L. Hix's liabilities was longer than that, and should have included dread sooner than it did. As eventually he recognized, since one feature of coming to dread something is seeing that you should have been dreading it all along.

•

What counts to ten in the morning, calculates compound interest at noon, sorts into multiples of seven in the evening?

•

All animals are fated, but some are more fated than others.

•

All shall be still, and all shall be still, and all manner of thing shall be still.

•

… shall dissolve and, like this insubstantial pageant faded, leave not a plastic bin of obsolete adapters and power cords behind.

•

Socrates is a human. All humans are mortal. Therefore,

H. L. Hix can't sit on the stool to shit, much less wipe his own ass.

• • •

H. L. Hix's dreams intensified during his illness, but they also expanded. He found it harder and harder to distinguish between dreams and hallucinations and waking life. Who knew how much of his soporific stupefaction was due to his illness itself and how much to the drugs prescribed against the illness? Who knew, and what did it matter? He came to feel as though he lived in a hypnagogic state, not intermittently but always.

At this moment, for example, H. L. Hix had long thick black hair, and he was sitting upright in an ornately-carved wooden armchair, like a throne but with only a shoulder-high backrest, rather than a tall one. He had his head tipped back slightly, to let his long black locks cascade down the back of the chair, and Prissy and Gary Simm, working together, were weaving his hair into one braid. Prissy was a man, and Gary Simm was a woman. Neither was looking at H. L. Hix's hair while they worked; instead, they were gazing deeply into one another's eyes. Both were adept at keeping the hair pulled enough to make a tight braid while handling very gently the not-yet-braided portion. As they took turns plaiting, they made sure to "accidentally" caress one another's hands. From the end of the loose, not-yet-braided hair, each time their hands touched, a snake dripped, like water dripping from a leaky faucet, and slithered away.

•

It was then, when it had become unclear where his dreams ended and his waking life began, unclear which of his experiences arose from perceiving what was there outside him, and which from hallucinating what was there only in his mind, that it became very *clear* to H. L. Hix that his kidney, the stonestruck debilitated and debilitating one, was speaking to him. The kidney spoke from inside him (it wasn't, say, floating before him like the dagger before Macbeth), but its voice came from outside. He felt it in one place and heard it in another, the way if you put a hand to your own chest or throat you *feel* your voice there even as you *hear* it outside you.

There was nothing for H. L. Hix to *see* for verification, but he didn't need to see the kidney to know that's what it was. No matter that it had never spoken to him before now, and didn't identify itself when it spoke: from its very first word, he recognized its voice. The kidney's voice was the voice of the brother H. L. Hix never had, blended with the voice of the daughter he never had. It bore a saturated echo, as if he were hearing it inside a cathedraled cave chamber, limelogged and lightless. It warped away from itself, as if it had carried from one shore to another over smooth morning lake water, through thick morning fog. It was flat, like lines drawn on paper in a configuration that suggests a volumetric cube but itself has no volume. It was coarse, as if it had taken on the texture of the cardboard paper-towel tube into one end of which it had been spoken while the other end was held tight to H. L. Hix's ear.

"You have measured out your life in table settings washed," the kidney declared to H. L. Hix. "Do the math. Bowl and spoon at breakfast, knife fork plate at dinner, meal after meal and day upon day for four decades. Here's a clue: the total's got five figures. You've worn out more dishrags than Cebes' soul-weary weaver has worn out woven cloaks.

Machine-made quasi-cotton squares from the dollar store, the party-colored pieces your Aunt Kack crocheted. Never mind the one-side-sponge-one-side-steel-wools you used to scrub the crust scalded onto casserole pans. You underlined a lot of passages from a lot of books, but the knowledge you'll take with you to your grave is how tenaciously the film from mozzarella melted into three-bean chili clings to a shallow stoneware bowl, and how much extra pressure it takes to clean the spot on the omelette pan where the teflon has worn away."

•

In his illness H. L. Hix had settled into the mental triple point at which dream, hallucination, and perception coexist, the point at which the observation curve, the imagination curve, and the delusion curve meet, the lowest point of mental function at which perception remains possible. This blurring of dream/hallucination/perception, their simultaneous presence, gave influence to Gary Simm, who often nudged H. L. Hix from one state to another.

"I can let you sleep through the nightmares if you want," Gary Simm offered on one occasion of his waking H. L. Hix. "I can let you sleep, but I woke you just now because you were kicking again, and this time you even raised your arms like you were stretching them out to grab something. You were calling out, and it sounded like you were screaming 'Oh! Oh!'"

"No, Gary Simm, don't leave me sleeping when I'm thrashing around." H. L. Hix's words came out slowly, thickly. Speaking felt to him now like walking through waist-high water. "Thank you for waking me. The nightmare did have me scared."

H. L. Hix had been dreaming about two women on horseback, riding side-by-side. The woman on the left rode a dark horse, the woman on the right a light horse. Each rider's clothes and hair matched the color of the horse she rode: dark for the rider of the dark horse, light for the rider of the light. He the dreamer saw them from behind. He was located just as if he were on horseback, accompanying them, a few steps back, or (because in the dream nothing of himself, not even his hands on the reins, or his own horse, not even its ears and mane, was visible to him) as if he were a camera following, keeping a consistent distance, filming the riders. The riders were familiars. The dreamed H. L. Hix knew them well. He knew who they were, and was riding *with* them. The dreaming H. L. Hix knew only *that* he knew them, but he didn't know who they were. He was only riding *after* them, not *with* them. The dreamed H. L. Hix could hear the hollow clopping of all three horses' hooves; the dreaming H. L. Hix could hear only the hooves of the other riders' horses, but not the hooves of his own.

They, all three, the two women with H. L. Hix close behind, were riding across a bridge high over a deep, steep-walled gorge. The bridge did not pass straight across the gap, but described a long curve sweeping out to the riders' left and back in toward their right. It was a roadway, not a walk-way, on concrete piers, with low concrete parapets (not metal guardrails) along the edges. The woman on the right, on the inside of the bridge's curve, was riding very close to the edge, close enough that even before anything had begun to happen, both dreamed and dreaming H. L. Hix were anxious, sens-ing something amiss, knowing before anything *did* go wrong that very soon something *would*. The woman riding near the bridge's edge leaned over very far, to look straight down onto the slender silver ribbon of river below. She leaned *so* far that she began to fall off her horse, and her horse, now overloaded to one side, began to tip over. Because they'd been so near the edge, when the horse tried to catch its balance, it did so by lifting its front legs over the abutment, to plant its hooves on that side, against its falling in that direction, but there was no bridge surface outside the abutment, nothing for the horse to plant its hooves on, so it began to pitch forward and to its right, over the bridge and into the gorge, throwing the rider even farther out, into freefall.

All this was happening in the dream in slow motion, extending the feeling of fear and futility as the dreamer, whose reactions were slowed just as much as what he was seeing, reached in vain toward the falling horse and rider. His hands weren't visible to him before the horse and rider began to fall, and didn't *become* visible to him during the fall, so he *felt* his arms stretching toward the falling figures, but did not *see* his arms reaching out.

In the bedroom, to Gary Simm's ears, H. L. Hix had been crying out "Oh! Oh!," but in the dream he had been pleading, in the *direction* of the falling horse and rider but *to* the rider still on the bridge, "No! No!" He was pleading *toward* the falling figures because the horse, pitched out far from the bridge and tumbling, now upside-down, now right-side-up, was growing smaller as it fell toward the impossibly distant floor of the gorge. In its falling the horse looked like a porcelain figurine, its four legs not flailing but held stiffly straight out. It looked like it would *keep* falling, getting smaller and smaller forever, the floor of the gorge receding as fast as the horse fell. The woman (in defiance of the laws of physics that govern the waking world) had fallen, once she was separated from her horse, back in toward the pier of the bridge, but not quite close enough to reach it. H. L. Hix was pleading *to* the figure still on the bridge because, even though he was watching the one woman fall, he was aware that the other was smiling and calm, and that somehow without moving she was actually controlling the other, first pushing her into her fall and then keeping her just out of reach of any hold that would slow or stop her falling.

•

The ottoman pose came as close as anything could to securing H. L. Hix in the "reality" that distinguishes itself from dream, but did little to settle him in the "reality" that differs from fiction. One afternoon, as they eased into the ottoman pose, H. L. Hix asked, "Are you just making up these stories you're telling me, or are they true?"

Gary Simm smiled broadly, and even chuckled quietly, before replying. "Are those my only two options?" H. L. Hix understood that he was being teased, but couldn't quite get a smile past the pain, to reformulate his question. Gary Simm didn't wait for an answer before continuing. "My Uncle Tito told a lot of stories. He lived with us for a stretch when I was a kid. Tito wasn't his real name, or even one that made much sense: he didn't have a drop of Italian or Spanish or Mexican blood in him. And he didn't *look* Mediterranean or Mexican, either. His face was a little pasty, and he had a swollen-looking, thickly-veined nose. Somebody at one of his jobs along the way started calling him Tito, and it stuck. He'd been a teetotaller for a while when he was young, but then he started drinking, and once he took to drink he drank a lot, so the name was a joke: he had the start of a teetotaller, but not the finish. My stories themselves might not all come from Uncle Tito, but my love of stories does.

105

"Once Tito started drinking, he wasn't much good at keeping a job, so he worked all over, doing different things, living different places. He tried sometimes to run something on his own. Once, he set up to take out stumps. He bought a beat-up, rusty stump grinder for ten bucks at a farm foreclosure auction, and hauled it home. It didn't work when he bought it, but he could fix things. He figured out how to get that rickety machine running, and how to replace the worn-down teeth. There aren't enough stumps in the whole world, though, to make a go of it doing stump removal alone, and you need a cherrypicker to trim trees, so the stump removing business didn't last long. That ten-dollar stump grinder went back to rusting, just off to the side of a different barn than the one it had sat rusting beside before Tito bought it.

"He lasted a little longer moving houses. Somehow he got hold of an old International Harvester Loadstar. It was funny how promptly loyalty kicked in, how proud he was of driving one of the early year-models, the kind that still had a butterfly hood. It had been bright red when it was new, but was dulled down in the direction of brown by the time he got hold of it, first from hard use and then from neglect. Working hard and being lazy, doesn't matter, either way you end up tired. (That was one of Tito's favorite sayings: he could use it to justify whatever he was doing.) Probably that truck was the same thing as the stump grinder: bought for nothing because it didn't much work, and nobody else wanted it, but Tito didn't mind a little rust and he could make any machine run. He didn't have any schooling, so he couldn't write or multiply, but he could eyeball anything. He replaced the stairs to the basement once when he was living with us: didn't draw up plans or measure how wide the treads should be and how high the risers, but everything fit just as if he had.

"The Loadstar, though, got lost to the one time Tito's usually reliable eyeballing was off. It happened out west somewhere — could have been right here in Wyoming, even. Or Utah. Someplace with more land than people, more rocks than trees. He'd loaded up a house. That much, he said, was easy: just cut the walls loose from pipes and such, get two beams under the floor joists, and slip a couple of good sturdy axles under the beams.

"What happened was he got out on the road and hit a snag halfway between where he'd taken the house from and where he was taking it to. He'd scouted the route he was planning, of course: even take-'r-easy-Tito thought that far in advance. He missed one thing, though: a guardrail at one T intersection that was too close for him to make the turn. So he backed up the truck, load and all, and just took off across a field to get from the east/west highway to the north/south one, but he didn't know that the *reason* it was barren, instead of planted with soybeans or overgrown with woods, was that not much grows on a gypsum sink.

"He didn't get far out into the field before the whole thing, the truck and the house together, was stuck, as if that field had been one of those runaway truck ramps. His way of dealing with it was pure Tito. He got hold of a pair of hundred-ton jacks from God knows where (and God knows who), and some good sturdy planks, and he pulled that truck free. But he just left the house right where it sat. Never towed another house, just took to doing something else. I bet that house is still sitting out there in that untended field, and nobody driving past even notices it, as if it had been built there and lived in for generations and then abandoned when the last one in the family line passed on. As if it were just part of the field, which by now it is."

•

H. L. Hix, sometime professor and writer, had devoted his full four decades of adult life to work he once had thought contributed to preparing others for life. Gary Simm, home health care aide and student nurse, barely two decades old, was, with altogether less pretension and self-deception, preparing others for death. One sought to maximize satisfaction, the other to minimize suffering. H. L. Hix delivered countless stiff, painstakingly prepared, tightly scripted lectures on matters of great pitch and moment, weighty subjects and weighty books; Gary Simm offered endless loose stories about this and that, all off the cuff. H. L. Hix's words were as burdened and burdensome as Gary Simm's were liberating and light.

H. L. Hix had believed in taking care, Gary Simm in giving it. Now, in their intimacy, Gary Simm's work was proving itself the more realistic of the two, much the more necessary, and by far the nobler.

dream [From the Proto-Germanic **draugmas*, deception or illusion, itself possibly a cognate of the Sanskrit *druh-*, to harm, and/or the Avestan *druz-*, to deceive.] A vision during sleep; the state in which this occurs; to have such a vision. In Caxton's summary account of Nebuchadnezzar (whose name he gives as Nabogodonosor), the sages and wise men of Babylon "coude not telle hym his dreme that he had dremed on a nyght."

Caxton there supplies one side of a double entendre here drawn out: H. L. Hix himself could tell his dreams, in the sense of "tell" that means to recount or narrate, but in the sense that means to interpret he was at a loss, not nearly sage enough to tell them.

•

As the air to a bird or the sea to a fish, so is death to the dead.

•

A spice that can be substituted for though no dinner guest notices, is not part of the savor.

•

All shall be veiled, and all shall be veiled, and all manner of thing shall be veiled.

•

… shall dissolve and, like this insubstantial pageant faded, leave not a dentist appointment reminder card behind.

•

Socrates is a human. All humans are mortal. Therefore,

H. L. Hix is given, at regular intervals throughout the day, pills he couldn't name and can't keep track of, the effects of which on his steadily weakening body he does not experience as distinct from the effects of the illness they are prescribed to combat.

•

"You have measured out your life in office windows. The shared fourth-floor window from which one afternoon you saw an angry cyclist pedaling alongside an upscale sedan use the chain of his bike lock as a whip to break one of the car's headlights. The single-hung window in the office on the converted floor of a dorm, through which each autumn you watched a ginkgo drop its every leaf in a single day, snowing around itself a perfect circle of perfect yellow. The antique window with its wavy glass through which you watched the demolition of an old building but not the construction of a new. The dormer window on the attic floor through which you could watch the grounds crew maneuver a zero-turn around the trees on a sqare of lawn, then trace that same lawn's sidewalk frame with a trimmer. The basement-office fixed-pane that let in light but looked out only onto a window well that gathered leaves and gum wrappers, and was visited often by squirrels but never by birds.

"You have measured out your life in committee assign-ments. The search committee that hired a colleague who within two years was fired for falsifying data. The promotion committee that waved away all the student evaluations that said one candidate never returned papers or exams, because he did bring in the grants. The curriculum planning subcom-mittee that reported to the strategic planning task force. The steering committee that could have used a little direction of its own. The visioning committee charged to research shared governance and, with input from focus groups, develop a Pythian Paper to 'guide our path forward.' The resource allocation working group that took away support from successful units, and assigned it to failing ones."

It was not that as his illness worsened H. L. Hix lost his memory altogether, just that the memories no longer came to him when he *wanted* to remember them, but instead imposed themselves unbidden. He could be listening to Gary Simm talking, and without noticing any transition find himself in some memory unconnected, or only very loosely connected, to his current context. This made the stone to H. L. Hix's kidney akin to consumption of the forbidden fruit in Eden, which after all must have been about the same size and shape as the culprit stone, and it brought H. L. Hix's mind into line with his paradigmatically post-lapsarian human body. He used to laugh at the passage in *City of God* that blamed Adam's one-time disobedience for the ever-after disobedience that makes the "organ of sex" so badly compromise the self-mastery of male humans, but nowadays he no longer found it funny. Adam, amid pear-burdened boughs, for dribbling a little fruit juice down his chin one time was punished, if Augustine could be trusted, with unwilled hard-ons for the rest of his days; H. L. Hix, amid dandelions grown up through driveway gravel, for passing an ill-maintained hardware-store power mower over his problem instead of solving it was punished with poisons accumulating in his thinning blood. Adam had been cursed with the little death, H. L. Hix with the big one.

Here, for example, mere thought of Augustine's pecker-fretted Adam led H. L. Hix to recall something he hadn't thought of for decades: the only time he had touched another man's "organ of sex." This was back in high school, when he'd been maybe fifteen. Very briefly (how long? a week? a whole semester?) there had been a quadriplegic fellow student. H. L. Hix no longer knew, if he ever had known, the cause of the quadriplegia: had this short-term friend of his been born without the use of his limbs? had disease taken it away? an accident? H. L. Hix did not remember, either, this friend's name, but did remember that a body cast encased his torso to help keep him upright in his electric wheelchair. And re-membered this friend as witty enough that, when it was H. L. Hix's turn to help the friend urinate (if this happened at all, why had it happened only once?), the friend, to whom of course the situation was routine, eased H. L. Hix's discomfort with some funny remark, probably the same remark used to lighten the situation for each first-timer. He could no longer recall the *mechanics* of the process: had the friend peed into a bottle H. L. Hix had held in place and then poured out? He only remembered the *fact* of touching — handling — some-one else's penis, and how troubling it had been for one whose upbringing had been intently focused on strictly limiting how often and in what ways and toward what ends he touched his own.

This unbidden memory only enforced on H. L. Hix one more way in which his illness and its symptoms deprived him of any possibility of self-affirmation. Why was *he* the one who needed consolation in either case, whether he was help-er or helped? Why, if he had needed the friend to ease his embarrassment then, did he also need Gary Simm to ease his embarrassment now, when the roles were reversed?

•

For what might have been only a moment, but seemed a long time, H. L. Hix was standing in a basement, bigger than the basement of his house, and built differently, but still it *was* the basement of his house. He had discovered that one whole wall was not secure: it did nothing to impede either human intrusion or invasion by vermin, and it could not long prevent collapse of the wall built above it. It was supposed to be built of sturdy concrete blocks, with two small window wells at the top to let in light, but in fact it wasn't *built* at all, just mounded out of loose dirt with three large openings (big enough to enter without stooping) dug through it into darkness. Each opening was covered only by a flimsy fake-bamboo plastic roll-up blind. H. L. Hix was trying to reconstruct the wall from wave-surfaced glass blocks, but the ones he had weren't all the same size, so he couldn't fit them together, and anyway he had no material with which to mortar them. Gary Simm and Priscilla Frederickson stood behind him, arms crossed, and any time he stood up, pausing in his attempt to build the wall, one of the two would give him a stiff shove between the shoulders to make him bend back over his work.

•

Again, as happened so frequently nowadays, H. L. Hix had to be awakened by Gary Simm, to end a bout of twitching limbs and twisted cries.

"What were you dreaming?" Gary Simm asked, in a voice that made it sound as if he were really interested, not just being polite. This was one of Gary Simm's gifts: an ability to do his job as if it weren't a job, as if he weren't working.

H. L. Hix paused for some time, to return more fully to a waking state before replying, and Gary Simm did not hurry him.

"I was dreaming." He began with this statement of the obvious, not to inform Gary Simm of something, but to reassure himself, to find his own footing. It was one symptom of his illness, that what he heard himself saying was more and more often farther and farther from what he'd meant to say, so anything (simplicity, triviality, …) that inclined intention and word toward rather than away from one another consoled him. "I was asleep in bed, but it wasn't quite me, and I wasn't quite asleep, and it wasn't *this* bed, or this room. The bed was bigger than this one, a lot bigger, and the room, which was much bigger than this room, was empty except for the bed. It was weird: somehow I knew, and for some reason it mattered, that the room was a perfect cube. That, the room's cubical shape, was the reason for my being there, and the condition for my being able to sleep. It was a square bed, with a very white sheet, and I was lying in the middle of it, on my back, naked. There was no top sheet, no blanket.

"At first, the dream felt very calm. I was sleeping peacefully. The sheet was clean and cool. I was clean and warm. In the dream, I wasn't dreaming. But then one bug crawled out from between my back and the sheet. It crawled across the bed and onto the floor. It was dark brown against the white sheets, a stink bug or a cockroach. Its antennae were as long as its body, and in a constant twitchy motion, feeling all around. 'Crawled' isn't quite right: it *scuttled*. Even its movement was repulsive. Repulsive to *see*: it looked jittery and germy, in a way that made me sick to my stomach. But repulsive to *hear* and *feel*, too: each step a tiny click but so rapid-fire that together they were raspy, as if I could feel the hooked tip of each leg catch on the cotton. I felt it in my fingertips in a way that sent a shiver, and I felt it in the back of my throat in a way that made me gag.

"Then another bug just like it crawled out from underneath me, and then another and another. Soon it was a whole swarm of dirty brown bugs, countless as bats at dusk from the mouth of a cave. It was a stream of bugs, flowing from a spring I was lying on top of but couldn't block. They flowed out all around me, covering first the whole bed and soon the whole floor. They were crawling over *me*, too, over my naked body, over my belly and my privates, into and out of my open mouth, over my open eyes."

Even in its badly weakened condition, H. L. Hix's whole body shifted uncomfortably as he narrated the dream. "There were too many of them for me to keep them off. I was swiping them away, but not nearly fast enough. I couldn't keep up. I was trying to get up, trying to get out, but I couldn't. When I moved to leave the bed, the smelly juice from crushed bugs stained the sheet, and when I walked across the floor trying to find the door — there *wasn't* a door to this room, and by now they were covering the walls, too — their shells crunched under my feet and the floor was slick with their innards."

Gary Simm, who had been listening patiently, without changing his facial expression, didn't speak, just nodded.

H. L. Hix paused only briefly before adding, "I don't know why I dream these things. They don't make sense, and *I* don't make sense. I can't keep myself from drifting off, but then my sleep isn't really sleep. I must look silly, kicking and mewing. But *all* my dreams are nightmares now, so it's always a relief when you wake me."

"It doesn't look silly when you stir," Gary Simm assured him with a calm smile, "but it is alarming. It makes *me* feel a little scared, too."

"They feel so real, all these nightmares, much more real now than anything in my waking life feels. More real than anything *felt*, back when I *had* a waking life."

After a long pause with no words between them, H. L. Hix continued, "Telling you about that dream reminds me of another dream I must have had a few days ago. Maybe I didn't stir during this one, because you didn't wake me. Or maybe I dreamed it while you weren't around. I had forgotten it until now. Or maybe my mind is making it up here and now." He paused again, having confused himself by introducing the possibility that he hadn't previously dreamed the dream he was about to report, but instead was about to dream it as he reported it, or that there was only the report of the dream, not the dream itself, or only a dream of the report. "I'm so addled these days, Gary Simm, so addled."

Gary Simm did not speak in reply, but gave a little nod and closed his eyes with a brief wince of sympathy.

Gary Simm knew to expect the delay that H. L. Hix was not aware of, between that admission and the resumption of telling about the dream. "I'd gotten up in the middle of the night to pee. Everything was familiar — it was this house — and I walked through the house in the dark, without stumbling or having to hold my arms in front of me. Like I say, it seemed real. But my face felt funny. It felt itchy. I felt itchy all over, but especially my face. When I got to the bathroom, I turned on the light, and I could tell in the mirror that there was something on my face. When I got up close, I saw there was a cluster of ticks at one corner of my mouth. They were the size and shape of lightning bugs, and they even glowed like lightning bugs, but they were ticks: their heads were burrowed into me.

"I squeezed the skin there, like squeezing a pimple, to pop them out one by one into the sink. Each one would then scurry away, and for some reason I didn't try to stop it. But they multiplied and spread. Every time I popped one out, two more would appear, burrowed into me somewhere else on my face. I kept popping them and popping them, and they kept crawling away, down the drain or over the lip of the sink and out across the bathroom floor, and more and more of them appeared."

•

Gary Simm offered his stories as diversion, a way to distract H. L. Hix from his pain and confusion, draw his attention away from his illness. Gary Simm didn't ask what they *meant*: why would he? For him, they were entertainment, a way to pass the time, not enigmatic oracles in which lay hidden the secrets of the universe and the meaning of life.

H. L. Hix did not *receive* them, though, in the same spirit in which Gary Simm *told* them. H. L. Hix and Gary Simm experienced time differently. For overflowing Gary Simm, time was abundant; for draining-away H. L. Hix, time was scarce. For Gary Simm, time spent could be replaced, would always be replaced, from an inexhaustible store, with more time, itself to be spent. For H. L. Hix, by contrast, time spent depleted a rapidly dwindling, severely limited store. Consequently, for Gary Simm no one story was any more than itself, no story was final, but for H. L. Hix any one story was every story, any story was ultimate. For Gary Simm, a story didn't *have* to mean anything: there would always be another story. For H. L. Hix, a story *had* to mean something: if it didn't mean something, it meant there was nothing.

For H. L. Hix, every story told the one story, the story of the death of H. L. Hix.

The difference in their stances did not make H. L. Hix *able* to discern meaning, much less *apt* at such discernment. His body too badly dulled his mind for that. He faded too often into and out of sleep to catch everything about a story, and he was too groggy and blurred to see outlines clearly. Still, he *tried*.

So when they next assumed the ottoman pose, with the familiarity and intimacy that Gary Simm seemed not even to notice but that each time nearly overwhelmed H. L. Hix, Gary Simm blithely began to tell a story that to him seemed random, simply the first that happened to come into his head.

"Have I ever told you about the owl?"

The surge of feeling — the relief from pain that the ottoman pose gave him, the sense of vulnerability from having his "private parts" exposed to another person, the shiver from the sensation of strong hands grasping his thighs — was powerful, like being lifted by an incoming wave, so H. L. Hix had to wait for the wave to pass, had to settle his feet back to the sand, before he could say in reply even a simple "No."

"There are lots of owl stories to tell," Gary Simm began. "Tito kept an owl once for a pet, a Great Horned Owl he'd rescued when it was small. It must have tried to fly too soon, and fallen from the nest. He found it out in the woods and brought it home and made a cage for it in the garage and fed it mice, but by the time it was full-grown, my father made him release it back into the woods. I don't know if you've ever seen one up close, but they're really *big*! And it's intense, the way they look at you. Dad and Tito both knew that owl wouldn't last long in the wild after being raised inside without learning to hunt, but I'm sure it was really my mother who'd insisted it had to go.

"After that, Tito whittled owl after owl. Each one was distinct, not because he carved them differently, but because each piece of wood was unique. He whittled a lot, maybe to keep his hands busy, maybe to keep them steady, maybe a little of both. His pocket knife was old: its bone handle was dingy and worn, but he kept that blade shiny and sharp. He bragged about how he'd won that knife in a poker game, and I don't doubt it: the blade was engraved with someone else's initials. I remember them: NKP. I used to go out and find good pieces of wood to bring him, partly so I could watch another owl emerge, but mostly because if you sat with him while he whittled, he'd start in on a story.

"But the pet owl isn't the story I was thinking of, much less the whittling. I was remembering a different owl that got into the house once in the middle of the night. This happened, too, when Tito was living with us. I don't know why so many stories involve Tito: he didn't really live with us that long. I guess because he *made* everything a story. But he was always in the middle of whatever was going on, and he was living with us when this owl showed up.

"Like I say, this was the middle of the night, everybody asleep, but my dad was a light sleeper. Because he had so much responsibility, to hear him explain it, what with two kids and his work and all. He'd had to teach himself to wake without an alarm when my sister and I were babies, he said, because the apartment we lived in at the time was small and he had to get himself to work without waking us. More likely, it was just him, just the way he was: he was going to be a light sleeper no matter what.

"Anyway, he, my dad, heard a stirring, so he got up to find out what was going on. Was one of his kids sick? Was Tito drunk? Had someone broken in? He went to the living room and located the sound in the dark, then turned on the light, but there was nothing there. That house had floor-to-ceiling curtains over the one window in the living room, even though it didn't need them: the window was a normal size picture window, not nearly floor-to-ceiling. Dad listened again for the stirring, and it was coming from the curtains.

"By this time, of course, *his* stirring and turning on lights had awakened the rest of us, so there we were, Dad in his boxers, that was what he slept in, me in my pjs rubbing my eyes, my mother in her housecoat and slippers, and Tito in nothing but a pair of jeans. I think he slept in his birthday suit, but my mother would have kicked him out then and there if he'd even once pranced around the house that way. My sister never heard a thing. If you called today and asked her, I bet she'd say it never happened. She'd tell you I was making up this whole thing.

"Anyway, Tito, being Tito, grabbed a poker from beside the fireplace, and had it ready, first holding one end and rapping the other end against his palm, then raising it over his head, like he was about to bash in the intruder's skull. Dad, being Dad, motioned Tito to wait, and went to the curtains and flung one side open.

"Of course the intruder wasn't a burglar. What was a burglar going to find in *our* house? It was an owl. Not a Great Horned, like Tito's outgrew-the-garage pet, but a little-bitty one, probably a Screech Owl. It must have gotten in through the flue, and then just couldn't find its way back out. We hadn't been in the house long: probably the previous tenants had left the flue open, and none of us had thought to check.

"We had a good laugh, first from relief, then from watching Dad and Tito try to catch the owl and take it outside.

They finally did release it, though not before Tito, holding that poor scared bird in both hands, teased my mother with it, saying we could keep it for a pet. In a cage in the kitchen, he laughed, and we could let it out each afternoon to circulate the air and supervise supper prep."

Gary Simm might have been telling the story "for no reason," because it was "the first thing that came into his head," but H. L. Hix didn't receive it that way. Maybe because of the medication, maybe despite it, the story, like all the stories Gary Simm told, seemed to H. L. Hix to be about *him*. In his hypnagogia, he couldn't keep his waking experience apart from his dreams, or his dreams from Gary Simm's stories. It was hard to tell them apart, and hard therefore to read them differently. Hearing Gary Simm tell about the owl felt, to H. L. Hix's already-blurry-and-getting-ever-blurrier mind, exactly like dreaming it for himself. He just knew, without being able to say why, that he *was* the house. He knew that the owl that entered through the flue and whose increasingly flustered flapping against curtain and pane flustered the whole household awake, was his illness, and that Tito's bemused release of the bird was his — H. L. Hix's — death. It didn't matter that Gary Simm couldn't possibly mean it that way, or that a younger, still-healthy H. L. Hix would have rolled his eyes at such a reading. It didn't matter that it wasn't how he would have thought about this story, hearing it in health: it was how he experienced the story now, in his illness. Comparing his understanding of things with others' understandings, and accounting for the differences between them, had mattered a lot then, to the living H. L. Hix, but now, to the already dead H. L. Hix, it mattered not at all.

"Gary Simm?"

"Yes. I'm here."

"Would you get me some water? I'm thirsty."

"Oh, I'm sorry. I hadn't noticed you were out."

Gary Simm picked up the tumbler. When H. L. Hix had first taken ill, Prissy had kept a glass tumbler on H. L. Hix's nightstand, but soon after Gary Simm had been hired, he discreetly replaced it with another the same size but made of colored plastic, to be more visible and thus less likely to be accidentally knocked over, and so that, if as he weakened H. L. Hix were to drop it, there would be only a spill and not also a shattering. Gary Simm had substituted a water bottle one day, to preclude spills, too, but H. L. Hix didn't have the strength to unscrew the cap, so Gary Simm had discreetly returned the plastic tumbler.

"Your breathing changed not long before you woke. Were you dreaming?"

Gary Simm left the room, refilled the tumbler at the kitchen tap, and returned. His walking away immediately after asking a question was not rudeness, simply knowledge that H. L. Hix, groggy in his uncertain return from sleep, would be slow to reply. Gary Simm helped him take a few sips, and then set the tumbler on the nightstand, within H. L. Hix's reach but at enough distance that it was unlikely to be knocked over inadvertantly.

"Thank you."

Gary Simm gave H. L. Hix a smile. "De nada." Gary Simm did not speak Spanish, but his pronunciation was good: not anglicized hard "d" sounds, but with his tongue farther forward, softening the d's toward "th."

He repeated his question. "So you were dreaming?"

"Yes. Of an old man, in bed, ill."

"You?"

There had been a time when he'd have teased Gary Simm about the unintended implications of his question, but H. L. Hix had long since lost the energy for banter, and lost, too, any interest in it. "No," he said without inflection, "it wasn't me. I was *watching* the scene, but from somewhere above or outside. I wasn't *in* the scene.

"The bed was ornate, with an intricately carved wooden frame and headboard. In the dream the figures, the people and the animals, were carved into the wood, but they moved. They were carved, but they were also alive. The bed had sheer white curtains around it. The old man was very thin and bony, all wrinkled and pale. I guess he was a lot *like* me, but he wasn't me. He had white hair, but I couldn't tell where his hair ended and the white pillowcase and sheets began. His hair grew out of his head, but it just *became* the bed linens. If he was me, he was a Rapunzel me. Come to think of it, he *was* locked away. Maybe the room wasn't in a tower, but it was locked from the outside.

"There were two nurses attending him, one on each side of the bed, but they seemed mechanical, like they were really robots rather than people: stiff movements, eyes focused a little too far away.

"The weird part of the dream, though, was that sometimes the bed would spin." H. L. Hix closed his eyes for a moment and furrowed his brow, trying to concentrate. "No, that's not it. It wasn't that the bed by itself was spinning. The whole house would spin, with the bed at the center of the spinning. The bed was the axis, or was at the axis. *That* was what was happening: the whole house was spinning around the bed, spinning with it, because of it. The whole *world* was. Every time the bed would start spinning, the man got more sick, and the nurses, who weren't affected by the spinning, would tend to him, but as he got more and more sick, their tending helped him less and less. It makes me queasy even now, just remembering the dream."

H. L. Hix paused long enough that Gary Simm asked, "So what happened?"

"Nothing. That was it. I woke up. Maybe it doesn't sound scary when I tell it, but it felt scary to dream it."

Another pause, but this time H. L. Hix broke the silence. "The old man only got sicker while I was dreaming, but he must have died when I woke up. Either his dying woke me, or my waking killed him."

•

By this stage of his illness, H. L. Hix was confined entirely to his bed, and the combination of his weakness, which left him unable to shift his own position, and his pain, which made lying on his back the least uncomfortable position, meant that he always faced the ceiling. Off to one side, a small stain spread across the ceiling away from the wall, shaped like Michigan growing out of Indiana. Directly above him, though, in his line of sight any time his eyes were open, was the smoke detector, a saucer-sized manila-folder-colored plastic butte with a tiny green LED test button glowing night and day.

The hypnotic, unblinking eye enforced on H. L. Hix the lack of control he experienced now over his own mind. If he wanted to think about the present moment, his memory would impose something from the past; if he wanted to engage Gary Simm in conversation, he would hear in his head someone else's voice, saying something that invited no reply. Under the light's influence, if he woke in the dark from the taste of pudding soured in his mouth, he would see, as clearly as if he stood slimed and sequined and stenched by them, a floodlit boat deck desperate with a net's worth of herring.

dusk [Of uncertain origin, but possibly from the Proto-Indo-European **dus-ko-*, dark-colored.] The darker stage of twilight. As given in Gavin Douglas, anything might *resemble* dusk: "The grund stude barrane, widderit, dosk, and gray." By contrast, to Kate Northrop, any one of us might *become* dusk, as when she reports being "quartered in this house, watching the neighbors' children / turn to dusk."

Here H. L. Hix discovers that he was always already dusk, "the twi-light of such day" as "blacke night doth take away, / Deaths second selfe that seals up all."

•

What gets diaper rash in the morning, poison ivy at noon, and bedsores in the evening?

•

All animals are doomed, but some are more doomed than others.

•

All shall be frail, and all shall be frail, and all manner of thing shall be frail.

•

… shall dissolve and, like this insubstantial pageant faded, leave not a graduation-gift set of monogrammed cuff links with a matching tie clasp behind.

•

Socrates is a human. All humans are mortal. Therefore, H. L. Hix, who once slept always on his side, now sleeps only on his back, to minimize the pain in his joints, especially his hips. The snot-bubble snoring from his stuffed sinuses creates an inharmonious counterpoint with the gag-gurgle from his mucous-marshed throat.

•

"You have measured out your life in laundry loads. They're far too many to *count*, but you can *calculate* how many garments you've draped over how many hangers, your solid-color shirts buttoning in one direction, Prissy's patterned blouses in the other. How many times the tennis ball knotted into a sock has knocked against the barrel of the tumble dryer. How many pairs of socks you've folded together into how many rabbits. How many dishrags you've accidentally dropped onto the unswept, seep-damp basement cement, lifting handfuls of clothes from the top-loading washer into the front-loading dryer. How many layers of how much lint you've swiped from the dryer filter, mostly cotton but just enough polyester that it can't be composted.

"You have measured out your life in wiper blades. 15-inch blades on both sides of the 1967 Dodge Dart you bought in college with what you could save from your part-time job lacing sneakers at the sporting goods store not far from campus. Slant six that slurped 10W30 fast as you please. Went splay-footed once when a tie rod worked itself loose. 19-inch blade on the driver's side, 17-inch on the passenger's side of the 1985 Toyota Corolla you bought the day you signed the contract for your first full-time job, that shivered the whole drive when you moved, tipsy from the car-top carrier bearing all your worldly goods, and that shivered once and for all years later, sandwiched between a station wagon in front and a pickup behind when some fool stopped on the on-ramp instead of merging. 22-inch driver-side blade, 18-inch passenger-side for the 1993 Honda Civic, in which you kept a shoebox on the floorboard, flush with mix tapes from friends. 20-inch driver-side blade and 18-inch passenger-side on the 2003 Hyundai Accent with a gravel-pitted windshield and a hail-pitted hood, that will still be parked on the street when your dandelion-seed soul drifts away on the breeze."

· · ·

"What was it this time?" Gary Simm could tell when H. L. Hix had wafted gently from peaceful slumber into what counted now as his waking state, and when he had been rudely shaken from fitful sleep by a nightmare.

"Another dream," H. L. Hix replied, without opening his eyes.

Gary Simm did not ask what he had dreamt; he waited quietly for the account, knowing it would come as soon as H. L. Hix had gathered himself.

"There was a lake, a big lake. You couldn't see the opposite shore. The whole surface of the lake was white, completely frozen over."

H. L. Hix paused, but this time Gary Simm spoke up. "And you were there?"

"Yes. And you, too. There was a fire on the shore of the lake. It wasn't the ocean, it was a lake, but the shore was wide and sandy, like an ocean beach. White. It wasn't just white sand, or snow-covered sand. Not one or the other, but both. It was sand *and* snow, at the same time.

"There was a fire, a big fire. It wasn't a bonfire, quite, not that big, but it was bigger than a campfire, and Prissy was standing by the fire, warming her hands at it. She would hold out her open hands to it and then rub them together and then hold them out again. Everything was reversed, though. Her face glowed, but it was brighter than the fire itself. It was her face that made the fire glow, instead of the other way around, and her hands that gave heat to the fire, instead of the other way around."

"And me?"

"You were stoking the fire. You would walk away along the shore of the lake and come back with a big driftwood log and lean it upright next to the fire and then tip it in. Really dropping it, so it sent up a big shower of sparks each time, and made a loud hiss."

"And this was scary?"

"Not the sparks and the hissing. What was scary was that the driftwood logs weren't really driftwood logs: they were my corpse, each of them. Again and again, you came back with my dead body and dropped it into the fire. You were feeding the fire with *me*."

•

When Prissy opened the door to H. L. Hix's room, she was sickened by the smell. He was lying inert, with his eyes closed, and did not react when she entered. He had soiled himself, and was lying in a dark puddle of his own liquidy pumpkin-pie-tinted shit, which stained the sheets, his gown, his sallow skin. Prissy called for Gary Simm.

"He's had an accident," she said, employing the same euphemism she would have used if he had been an infant or a puppy. "Can you help me change his sheets and get him cleaned up and changed into another gown?"

H. L. Hix lashed out, "Leave me alone! You weren't there to prevent the problem, don't pretend now to fix it!"

"I'm sorry to have to say this," Gary Simm said to Prissy, "but we should check his pulse." Without giving any sign of being disgusted by the stench, Gary Simm approached the bedside and held H. L. Hix's wrist, not for a full sixty seconds to get an accurate count, but long enough to report, "The pulse is slow, but he's still alive."

H. L. Hix's mind, so soggy for so long, felt suddenly parched. "Get away from me," he demanded. His voice, so long weak, felt suddenly strong. He shouted, "You can't sanitize this. This is how it will happen. My heart will stop beating and still I will shit. Let me die this way. Let me die now."

"Tell me we're nearing the end of this ordeal," Prissy pleaded to Gary Simm.

"I think we are. He's unresponsive, so he's probably in the coma the doctor said was likely."

H. L. Hix's mind, so smudgy for so long, felt suddenly clear. But this renewed clarity of mind only confronted him with puzzlement. What if my life was, and now my death is, utterly ordinary? What if the most ordinary thing about me was that I thought I was not ordinary, tried desperately not to be ordinary? If the most uniform, most universal, thing about me was my thinking myself unique? What if the very thing I saw about others, that they couldn't distinguish real from fantastic, was exactly what I didn't see about myself? If my only seeing it in others was one manifestation of its being in me? If I kept trying to make my inner life and my outer life match, but there never *was* an outer life? Or, worse, never an inner life? What if there *isn't* a reality for my fantasy to submit to? If the thought that there is a reality is one feature of my fantasy, the most fantastic fantasy? What if the more I struggled against hypocrisy the more tightly I was caught in it? What if the falseness of the false doesn't imply the trueness of the true, but only indicates that *everything* is false, only *makes* everything false? What if my whole life has been false, and the most false thing about it was my pretense — my delusion — that I could secure something true?

"I can clean him up," Gary Simm said to Prissy. "You don't have to stay for this. You can take comfort. If he's in a coma, then he's not in pain, he's already at peace."

Gary Simm's assurance did console Prissy, but did not accurately describe H. L. Hix's condition. He was unresponsive to them, he did appear to them to be in a coma, but it would have been more apt to say his awareness had shifted out of phase with theirs. His experience was not in sync with theirs, not in contact with it. While Gary Simm was assuring Prissy that H. L. Hix was at peace, H. L. Hix, or someone who, to H. L. Hix, resembled H. L. Hix, was gesturing to a spot just behind Prissy as she approached him. He was standing on their front stoop, holding open the storm door. She was on the walk, returning home, nearing the door. "Close the gate behind you," he was saying. She had left the front gate open when she entered their yard. There was no wind, but the gate was swinging back and forth, as if there were strong gusts, testing the hinges. "Close the gate behind you," an increasingly frustrated H. L. Hix repeated, but Prissy seemed not to hear, and did not respond. "Close the gate behind you," H. L. Hix kept saying, with increasing exasperation but to no avail.

"Close the gate behind you."

dust [From the Germanic **dunstu-*, and thus more ultimately from the Indo-European **dhwens-*, to dissipate.] Solid matter, disintegrated into particulate form. To which condition, according to Genesis, we humans long ago were once and for all consigned by very God: "In the sweat of thy face shalt thou eat bread, till thou return unto the ground; for out of it wast thou taken: for dust thou art, and unto dust shalt thou return."

From H. L. Hix's never having doubted those words it does not follow that he ever believed them. For *that* to happen, he'd have to disprove the more perplexing declaration from the Duke in *Measure for Measure*: "Thou art not thyself, / For thou exists on many a thousand grains / That issue out of dust." There'd have to have been a *himself* to do the disproving.

•

The death of H. L. Hix can never be told so as to be understood, and not be believ'd.

•

A joist that can rot through though no subfloor sags and no roof collapses, is not part of the structure.

•

All shall be nil, and all shall be nil, and all manner of thing shall be nil.

•

… shall dissolve and, like this insubstantial pageant faded, leave not a jelly jar of long-since-useless keys behind.

Socrates is a human. All humans are mortal. Therefore, H. L. Hix's ankles are so swollen from buildup of fluid that he would be bothered by their tenderness if he weren't feeling so much more pain in so many other parts of his body.

•

"You have measured out your life in living quarters. Never mind your bedrooms as a boy, a first few shared with your sisters before a last few of your own, but none of them your choosing. Never mind your bunk-bedded, double-desked, outdated dorm rooms in school. There was the second-floor shambles you shared for six months with the shit who didn't wipe the toilet rim after he pissed or swish out the sink after he shaved. Followed by the studio apartment, a badly-renovated motel room, its toy refrigerator filled exclusively with your own past-date milk turning sour and your own cardboard carrier still taking up a six-pack's worth of space on the shelf despite being down to one last beer. There was the up of an up/down duplex, with a sliding glass door as one wall of the bedroom, that opened onto nothing, no terrace or deck, but did give a good view of the single mother who lived downstairs, when she set out the webbed beach lounger and lay sunbathing in the back yard. And that doesn't count your houses, like the "airplane bungalow" with the upstairs room that shivered in storms and, once, from an explosion six miles away. The houses, all the gravity furnaces filling whole basements, all the badly do-it-yourselfed add-on rooms and the incessantly clinking pull chains under badly out-of-balance ceiling fans."

∙ ∙ ∙

Even out-of-phase awarenesses can at points intersect. With no initiating cause Priscilla Frederickson or Gary Simm could point to, H. L. Hix began what proved to be three days of ceaseless keening, so shrill that, even with the windows closed, the neighbors had to suffer it. "No!," H. L. Hix screamed, "No!," over and over, drawing out each "o" longer than should have been possible to one whose phlegm-filled lungs were failing. "No-o-o-o-o!"

For those three days the struggle was constant. To describe it as something he saw in his imagination or thought in his mind would imply a lucidity long lost, irrecoverably lost, to him. Instead, the conflict was something H. L. Hix felt in his limbs and viscera, an experience that replaced anything previous, death changing *what* he suffered by changing *how* he suffered. He was no longer a human person, an integrated self. The struggle had transformed him into the litter of frantic kittens in a croker sack, its darkness as final as his flailing was futile, nothing to do but claw, nothing to claw at but himself.

H. L. Hix's death, like every human death before his and every death to follow, was a death worse than a fate worse than death. His departure was absolute, absenting himself from himself utterly, but without at all compromising the wholeness of the whole. His no longer being himself did not make anything else no longer itself. His no longer *being* did not one whit diminish Being. *His* universe was taken from him fully and finally: nothing for him to experience, no *him* to experience it. *The* universe remained the universe, the wholeness of the whole no less whole for having excluded him, the nothingness of nothingness no less nothing for having subsumed him.

The caught kittens' clawing stopped — was stopped — with a sudden blow, as if the bearer of the sack had swung it hard against hard ground. The blow brought the burst of pain that broke pain open: no more pain, because nothing but pain.

When the clawing within stopped, so did the crying out. Prissy and Gary Simm rushed into the room. Gary Simm took H. L. Hix's wrist: still a pulse, however weak. He nodded at Prissy. They stood, one on H. L. Hix's left, one on his right, each holding one of his bony hands. They looked at each other, not down at him.

H. L. Hix's eyes were closed, but he saw Priscilla Frederickson and Gary Simm standing at the bedside. He told them both to leave, but neither moved. "Go away!," he said, but they did not hear him. He said it again, more urgently, but though he was fairly yelling his voice grew no louder. Still his closed eyes saw them standing there, and still, in the increasing distance from his body that was a sinking under his body, he felt them holding his hands. He pulled his hands away, but they did not move, were not released by his caretakers' grasp.

Gary Simm and Prissy listened to H. L. Hix's breaths grow noisier even as they weakened. Prissy did not say out loud that H. L. Hix's raspy breaths sounded to her like a straw-bristled broom arrhythmically swept over scuffed hardwood. Gary Simm kept to himself his thought that H. L. Hix's labored breathing sounded like a small child scooping little handfuls of gritty dirt into a coffee can.

The moment of death offered H. L. Hix no vision of light. The moment of death was not a moment. His awareness ended well before his breathing ceased. Prissy and Gary Simm could not have identified the former ending, but recognized the latter: a faint percussion echoed through H. L. Hix's hollow chest, the flapping of the last bat departing a cave, attended by the slightest shudder.

"It's over," Gary Simm declared to Prissy, or Prissy to Gary Simm. There was no H. L. Hix to tell which, or to care, no H. L. Hix to say as last words to himself, "Life is over. Death is over."

He did not at that moment breathe his last breath and die, having breathed his last breath just before then, being already dead.

www.ingramcontent.com/pod-product-compliance
Lightning Source LLC
Chambersburg PA
CBHW021734190726
48288CB00009B/3035